MONSTER HUNTERS UNLIMITED

MAN-MONSTERS AND ANIMAL HORRORS

BY JOHN GATEHOUSE AND DAVE WINDETT

PSSI
PRICE STERN SLOAN
An Imprint of Penguin Group (USA) LLC

For Steve & Kate, Adam & Kerry, and Emma & Dan.
And for Lucky Cat, the most terrifying Animal Horror
of them all! (No, really! He is!)—JG

To The Raptus (Norway) and
Wicked (Malta) Comics crews—DMW

PRICE STERN SLOAN
Published by the Penguin Group
Penguin Group (USA) LLC, 375 Hudson Street, New York, New York 10014, USA

USA | Canada | UK | Ireland | Australia | New Zealand | India | South Africa | China

penguin.com
A Penguin Random House Company

Library of Congress Cataloging-in-Publication Data is available.

ISBN 978-0-8431-6994-2   10 9 8 7 6 5 4 3 2 1

INTRODUCTION

When I'm asked "Are you afraid of the dark?" my answer is "No, I'm afraid of what is in the dark."

—Barry Fitzgerald (born William Joseph Shields, 1888–1961)

—Irish stage, film, and television actor

There is no escape from the dark. It is everywhere.

In detritus-filled alleyways overrun by vermin. In abandoned buildings and dank sewers. In the woods and the forests. Darkness exists below the seas and in the skies above.

Darkness skulks within your school locker and inside your wardrobe and under your bed.

And wherever there is darkness, so, too, there are . . . **MONSTERS!**

Hellions and devils, vampires and were-beasts. Putrefying zombies and murderous fae folk. Abominable man-monsters, hideous animal horrors, ghosts, ghouls, flying freaks, and perverted aberrations of unnature. These are Satan's children and the progeny from the Dark Dimensions.

Monsters are found worldwide. They hide in the dark places, waiting to prey on the weak, the helpless, the unsuspecting, and the disbelievers.

These creepoids are savage, merciless—their attacks are as swift as they are deadly! Blood-slurping, bone-crunching, eyeball-squishing, they suck out the brains and feast on the fresh entrails of humanity!

If a monster has you in its sights—there is NO escape!!

Lucky then, for the miserable mewling masses of mankind, that there is a band of kick-ass, insane-in-the-membrane warriors willing to risk death and dismemberment (and various other nasty demises) to protect them!

Monster hunters are a rare breed. We know no fear! (And occasionally, not much sense, either!)

While others quiver in pathetic, pants-wetting terror behind locked and bolted doors (which won't stop a homicidal ghost intent on dealing death and destruction, we hasten to point out), members of the International Federation of Monster Hunters take the fight to the monsters!

Our motto: No Surrender!

If slicing 'n' dicing a rampaging zombie and going mano a mano with a berserker ogre rocks your boat, you've come to the right place!

We're going to help you get a rep as one of the greatest monster hunters of all time! (It sure beats that recent math test you took—and if you flunk out, you won't be grounded for not studying hard enough! You'll just be, um, "grounded." As in, six feet under!)

What you hold in your hands is a monster hunter's most important possession. The information found within is totally intense!

You'll discover the weird and wacky world outside of the norm. A senses-shattering separate plane of existence inhabited by the maleficent macabre monstrosities and psychotic paranormal phenomena that rampage across this planet—the likes of which no sane person can possibly imagine!

The renowned to the esoteric (those you've never heard of!), the omnipotent to the embarrassing (yep, some monsters are *really* embarrassing!! Such as? Well, how does the knee-knocking Were-Snail grab you?! Or the not-so-dreaded Groke, the giant blue blob! Oooh! Scary!).

But for every dweeb monster, there are a kazillion others that will most probably have you kicking up the daisies unless you follow our advice!

The unstoppable Disemboweler for one! (Three guesses what this flipped-out female does for fun!) And the vomit-inducing Nuckelavee, the flayed man-horse (whose skin has been completely stripped from his body! *Icckk!!*).

Before setting out on your monster hunts, we'll supply you with the latest intel about each of the freaked-out therianthropes and crazed cryptids you're going to be facing!

Their origins, locations, appearance, strengths, weaknesses, powers, and Fear Factors!

That's! Not! All! Each chapter lists the various types of weapons and techniques you'll need to track down, capture, and—if necessary—*destroy* your prey! (Trust us, you'll need to destroy them before they destroy *YOU*!)

Don't forget to pack the old reliables, such as the wooden stakes, silver bullets, electromagnetic detectors, PKE meters, magic incantations, religious artifacts, swords, and battle-axes!

Our case studies reveal other humans' encounters with these fetid, foul, feculent fiends! Transcripts from a flight data recorder, a radio news broadcast, and a monster movie script; monster hunters' blogs and diary entries; a twisted online protest group trying to protect the vampiric giant owl, the Strix; ancient parchments; top-secret government files; web pages; downloads; and dozens more!

Don't keep your epic conflicts with these death-dealing grotesques to yourself! Each time you encounter a gnarly man-monster or bloodthirsty animal horror, send us your reports, smartphone photos, drawings, film recordings, diary and tablet entries, blogs, and tweets, plus your own genius ideas for battling and defeating them!

We've rated each of these beasts of night and shadow, from the most deadly to the utterly laughable! Agree with our assessments? No?! Then make your own Monster Fear Factor Top 10 for each section of the book!

Hunting monsters isn't for the wimps and wimp-hearted! Only the bravest of the very brave can apply to join the International Federation of Monster Hunters!

Got what it takes? Then check out the nasties covered in these pages and go kick some monster butt!

DISCLAIMER: Anyone who goes monster-hunting does so at his or her own risk. We cannot be held responsible for our readers turning into vampires, werewolves, zombies, or assorted baddies.

TABLE OF CONTENTS

MAN-MONSTERS

You gain strength, courage, and confidence by every experience in which you really stop to look fear in the face.

—Eleanor Roosevelt (1884–1962)—First Lady of the United States of America from 1933–1945, human-rights activist

Pop quiz! Who's the most famous man-monster of all time? *Pfft!* Like even a wet-behind-da-ears newbie is going to get that one wrong!

But for those of you who think the Frankenstein dude is real, sorry to piddle on your parade, but—he isn't!

We know, shocker. (Hey, some losers reckon the great Victorian detective Sherlock Holmes really existed! Roll-of-eyes time! *Snort!*)

Frankenstein; or, The Modern Prometheus (published in 1818) was a terrifying (and freak-the-mind brilliant!) über-Gothic horror novel written by English writer and essayist Mary Shelley (1797–1851), in a time when most female novelists were scribing, to put it mildly, pass-the-bucket soppy romance pap! (Shelley's book is considered by many to be the first true science-fiction novel!)

And the title character wasn't the monster itself, but twisted scientist Victor Frankenstein, who stitched up leftovers of rotting corpses to create a sorta-living abomination! Bodacious!

But that doesn't mean that for-real man-monsters (and woman-monsters!) don't exist! They do! The trail of eviscerated (stomachs ripped open, giblets pulled out!), mangled corpses across the globe attest to this gruesome fact!

And you're going to be hunting these gross-out suckers—and taking them down!

On your to-do list are epic battles with mega-size human-chomping ogres and giants!

The English psycho witch hag Black Annis! Harionago, the Japanese femme fatale, she of the writhing snake hair! And skeletal Russian nightmare Koschei the Deathless—the monster who cannot die!

But the mind-twisting horrors don't end there! Oh no!

We'll also introduce you to those vicious human-animal hybrids, creatures that combine body parts to create a flesh-eating, blood-guzzling freak show supreme!

The totally *eeev-iiilll* and sadistic sorcerous man-goat, the Mayan Huay Chivo! The dog-headed human barbarian warrior Cynocephalus! And the heartless woman-lion Sphinx, she of the deadly death riddles!

But what about the totally crazy Therianthropes?! They're our favorites!

For those among us who cut paranormal class, get with the program! Therianthropy is the ability to metamorphose from human to animal, and this kooky-but-kind-of-cool supernatural ability is one of the oldest on record!

You want proof? Take a trip to the ancient cave of Trois Frères ("Three Brothers") in Ariège, France, and enter a deep interior chamber known as "the Sanctuary."

There, you'll eyeball over 280 late-Paleolithic cave paintings dating back some fourteen thousand years, one of which depicts a shaman transforming into a stag with antlers!

This highly detailed painting, named *The Sorcerer* by archaeologists who discovered it in 1914, is the only one of the engravings painted all in black.

Is this the first recording of early man's ability to shape-change? You tell us!

We have some phenomenal, far-out theriolater (animal worshipping) Therianthropes to serve you up, including the mentalicious Mediterranean man-donkey Onocentaur and everyone's numero uno monsters of choice, the dreaded were-beasts! (Well, were-snails aside, that is! They suck, big time!)

It's kind of obvious, but even though this section is called *MAN-Monsters*, a fair share of the freaked-out freakzoids we're going to cover are actually female! (And believe us, these demonic dudettes are even more dangerous and psychotic than the dudes!)

Case in point: Meet the bloodthirsty strangler known as—Al! (Bit of a dorky nom de guerre—French for *war name*, i.e., a person's pseudonym, handle, or tag—we readily admit, but are YOU going to take her up on it?! Didn't think so!)

!!WARNING!! Those of an extremely nervous disposition should probably skip this chapter. Things are about to turn decidedly GRUESOME! Yeah, we know—mental!

Way back when, in the ancient kingdoms of Armenia and Parsa (aka Persia), an Al was described as being half-animal, half-human, with a hairy monkey-type body, snakelike hair, fiery eyes, a clay nose, iron teeth, brass fingernails, and a pair of huge boar tusks. Oh, and they come tooled up with a pair of enormous scissors!

(History note: 2,500 years ago, Parsa was the most successful of the 240 kingdoms in Iran. The kings of Parsa eventually created the largest empire the world had known to that date, what we call the Persian Empire.)

In Iran, those fortunate to survive a meeting describe Al as a bony, thin old woman with a clay nose and a red face who carries a reed or straw basket on her shoulder.

"No, they're not!" cry out the irate people of Afghanistan. "An Al is a young lady with long-flowing hair, razor-sharp talons, and backward-facing feet!"

And in Asian countries, Al appears as an ugly, fat, hairy crone who carries a woolen sack over her shoulder!

Whatever form they may take, the Al serve their king, who lives in the abyss (a deep chasm). This demonic dude is chained and sprinkled up to the neck in molten lead, which kind of hurts and makes him shriek continually in anger.

Wait, wait, wait, we hear you snort. This chapter isn't so gruesome!

Oh, ye of little faith! (You should know us by now!)

Al have an almighty hate-on for pregnant women, new mothers, and babies.

During childbirth, they will attack the mother; scorch her ears; use their scissors to tear out her lungs, liver, and heart (which they then carry away in their basket or sack); and strangle both mom and baby!

An Al may also steal a baby of forty days old and replace it with an imp (a demon child!).

Or cut out an unborn child of seven months from the womb and make it deaf and dumb, as a tribute to their king.

If it's feeling particularly mean, it'll poison the unborn child with hideous diseases, turn it blind, and suck out its brain and blood before eating its flesh!

Oh, and they also have a taste for rotting human corpses!

Is *that* gruesome enough for you?!

Case Study 039/67A

The Crusades were a series of bloody wars that took place across Asia Minor and the Levant between AD 1095 and AD 1291.

It was basically the Christian Roman Catholic Church versus the Saracens (the European word of its time for people of the Muslim faith) for control of the city of Jerusalem and the Holy Land, and each side did many terrible deeds to the other.

There were nine Crusades in all, and although the Christians were top dog for a time, they were eventually defeated and sent packing.

Here is an eyewitness account written by an unnamed knight during the First Crusade. It tells of the Christians' storming and capturing of Jerusalem in what became known as the Siege of Jerusalem (June 7–July 15, 1099):

I exult with joy! After five bloody weeks of battle, the gates of the holy city are open to us.

It happened most quickly once my good friend Letholdus climbed to the top of the wall, scattering the defenders with powerful thrusts of his sword.

Once we had gained entrance, we chased the terrified Saracens through the streets, hacking, slashing, and cutting them down without mercy.

At the Temple Mount, ten thousand did cower: men, women, and children, and not one did we spare. Our feet to our ankles turned red with their lifeblood.

Our commander ordered a group of us to search the darkened backstreets for anyone not already dead or captured.

Letholdus and I soon sighted what we assumed was an old hag in the shadows, and called out to her to surrender, promising that no harm would thus befall her.

But this was no mere washerwoman! She was the devil's spawn in human disguise! Both human and animal, she had the hair of serpents; thick, hairy flesh; fiery eyes; and two enormous tusks that sprouted from the corners of her mouth!

With a cry of rage, she rushed at Letholdus, brandishing the largest scissors ever crafted!

Raising his sword for combat, Letholdus was thus open for attack. Opening the scissors wide, the creature swiftly shut them around his neck!

His head came loose from his body, blood gushing like a fountain from his neck stump!

Before I could recover from my shock, the creature had disappeared back into the shadows!

AL FACT FILE

Location: Middle East, Central Asia, and the Caucasus (a geopolitical region that includes part of Russia, Iran, and Georgia, among others)
Appearance: Human-monkey-boar combo!
Strength: Terrifying!
Weaknesses: Magic spells, charms, prayers, iron objects, garlic, and . . . um . . . onions! (We know, sad!)
Powers: Razor-sharp scissors
Fear Factor: For pregnant women and newborns—100!!!

HOW TO DEFEAT AL

Challenge her to a game of rock-paper-scissors. Since she will only be able to play scissors, you play rock and you'll always win!

Oh, c'mon! Get real! We could hardly do a section on Man-Monsters and forget the daddy of them all—Bigfoot!

Most folk reckon Bigfoot to be the "wild hairy man of the forests" from the legends of the tribes of the Pacific Northwest region of the United States.

Don't bet on it! Sightings of such creatures have been reported worldwide and for thousands of years!

In Canada, they are known as Sasquatch; in Australia, Yowie. People of the Basque Country in the north of Spain call them Baxajaun or Basajaun.

Vietnam has the Rock Apes, and in Iran, the Ghool Biabony! (Love that tag!)

The first reference to this savage cryptid appears in the epic poem from ancient Mesopotamia (an area covering modern-day Iraq, the northeastern part of Syria, a squidgin of Turkey, and even less of Iran) entitled *Epic of Gilgamesh*.

The original poems (which were part fact and part fiction) were separate stories rather than parts of an actual poem. They were written on clay tablets by scholars living in the Neo-Sumerian Empire (aka the Third Dynasty of Ur) in southern Mesopotamia around 2150 BC to 2000 BC.

The later version, cobbled together by the Akkadians, consisted of twelve tablets that were edited around 1300 BC to 1000 BC.

(FYI: Akkad is considered by many historians as the first true empire in history, lasting from 2350 BC–2150 BC; it was wiped out by, of all things, climate change! Go figure!)

In the poem, the hero Gilgamesh befriends the wild man Enkidu, who is described as being shaggy with "hair that sprouted like grain." Enkidu ate with the gazelles and drank at water holes with the wild beasts!

No matter which continent or country, descriptions of Bigfoot are almost uniformly the same.

For starters, he isn't called Bigfoot because of his elephantine ears!

Footprints have been measured that reach at least two feet (sixty centimeters) in length and eight inches wide, with anywhere from two to six toes!

The hairy creature is between six and ten feet tall, and carries roughly five hundred pounds of body weight! (Oooh! Time to join Weight Watchers, dude!)

A low-set forehead and conspicuous brow ridge (aka the *supraorbital ridge*, the bony ridge above the eye sockets of all primates), flat nose, and long arms finish off his deformed features. Oh yeah, and he stinks—gross squared!

These pug-uglies communicate with one another by using a series of grunts, whistles, and gestures. Some are shy and retiring (ahh!) while others will rip you apart without a second thought!

Case Study 522/11B

Some imbecilic mokes out there reckon it's kind of "cool" to hunt down and kill defenseless animals for "sport."

These All Brawn and No Brain-ers like to boast about their kills in popular hunting magazines and on websites.

Here's one hunter's report in the most recent issue of *Kill-Zone* about a hunt that didn't quite go as planned.

The Hunter & the Hunted

by Frank Leedum

My pa taught me my love of the kill when I was eight, and now was the time to blood my own son Joel.

The kid had already practiced shooting targets with the .243 rifle I'd given him for his tenth birthday, but if he were ever to become a Real Man, he needed his first tag credit!

So one day midsummer last, we headed out to the Oregon wilderness for some whitetail deer hunting. It was a day he would never forget!

Dressed in an orange hunter jacket, and with his goofy grin and cheerful "Yee-ha," he sure did look the part!

Making our way on foot along the track of Snake River, dividing rugged mountains and rolling plains, with its tall timber, grassy slopes, and abundant hawthorn bushes, we moved stealthily upwind through the pines.

Then——it happened!

"Pa!" hissed Joel, pointing to where a huge brown shape was crashing noisily through the undergrowth. "Grizzly!"

Impossible! The last grizzly was hunted and killed in Oregon in the late 1930s. It had to be a black bear!

Finger to lips, I signaled Joel to follow me forward. His first kill was going to be a bruin!

Big mistake! The creature that faced us sure weren't no bear! Thick hair matted its face and body, and its feet were ginormous!

"Bigfoot!" I gulped, raising my own .375. "Wait until the guys at the lodge see this kill!"

But no dice! Rushing forward at impossible speed, Bigfoot wrenched the rifle from my grip, tearing off my trigger finger in the process! Man! The agony was intense!

Roaring angrily, the monster twisted the barrel into a knot before tossing it aside!

Blinded by pain from my lost digit, I had no chance of stopping the creature from snatching up the terrified boy and disappearing into the undergrowth. My kid was never seen alive again.

It was a day Joel would never forget, all right—his last!

BIGFOOT FACT FILE

Location: Forests, worldwide
Appearance: Tall, hairy, big feet—you'll know him when you see him!
Strength: Can bench-press your mom's car without working up a sweat!
Weaknesses: Knotted hair (aka trichonodosis). If you've ever suffered from the same, you'll know why! It hurts!
Powers: Can choke you to death with his puke-inducing BO, or crush you with his bare hands. Can reach speeds of up to thirty-five miles per hour!
Fear Factor: 42.6

WHAT TO DO WITH A CAPTURED BIGFOOT

Hire him out to a hairstyling academy as a model to practice on!

BLACK ANNIS

BRITISH CA...

Anywhere underground that someone needs help

Home   Links   Welcome   Register   Log in

Key Information

Cave Survey
Caving Gear
Caving News
Conservation
Site Information
Uncategorized

Recent Posts

Cave Closure Order
Training Days
Fund-raising

Black Annis's Bower

WEDNESDAY 20 MARCH at 14:25
(for 3 ¾ hours) (17 Team Members)
A twenty-seven-year-old registered "monster hunter" fell down a crevice while
investigating the infamous Black Annis's Bower" and became tightly jammed
between rocks. Numerous attempts to pull him free ended in failure because
the rope mysteriously broke each time. (more)

B.C.G.

Here's part of a poem written in 1797 by John Heyrick, an English army lieutenant in the Fifteenth Regiment of Light Dragoons. (Don't sweat it. It's cool!)

Tis said the soul of mortal man recoil'd,

To view Black Annis' eye, so fierce and wild;

Vast talons, foul with human flesh, there grew

In place of hands, and features livid blue

Glar'd in her visage; while the obscene waist,

Warm skins of human victims close embraced.

Hardcore! And no, he wasn't writing about his dear old mam, but that most hideous of cannibalistic and wizened hags, Black Annis!

This nighttime beauty is also known by the handles Black Anny, Black Anna, Black Agnes, Cat Anna, or Cat Annis; the latter two because of her neat ability to turn into a cat.

With her blue skin, one eye, razor-sharp teeth, and long, black iron claws that can cut through almost anything, Black Annis kind of stands out in a crowd in the leafy shires of the county of Leicestershire in the United Kingdom.

Many centuries ago in Leicestershire's Dane Hills, Black Annis used her powerful iron claws to cut through solid rock to create her own home-sweet-home cave.

Fearful locals named this cave Black Annis's Bower, and sensibly kept their distance. For whenever an animal or human passed by, Black Annis would leap out of hiding and gleefully eviscerate them!

King Richard III (1452–1485) of England had quite an unfortunate run-in with Black Annis on his way to battle Henry Tudor, Earl of Richmond (1457–1509), at Bosworth Field in Leicestershire on August 22, 1485.

His spur accidentally struck a stone pillar on Bow Bridge. This so infuriated Black Annis that she put a death curse on Richard, declaring that it would be his *head* that hit the post on his return journey.

Sure enough, Richard was one of the 1,100 fatalities of the battle, which saw around 21,000 soldiers hacking and slashing each other with sharp swords and battle-axes, leaving said field awash with blood.

The now ex-king's naked body was slung over a donkey, and on the way home his head did indeed whack that very stone!

The Dane Hills were flattened in the last century in the name of "progress," so Black Annis simply moved the cave underground!

Although she will happily chomp down on human adults and farm animals, especially lambs, her favorite snack is the soft, juicy flesh of young children.

Snatching kids from inside the safety of their homes, she drags the screaming brats to her cave, hangs them up by their arms, and slowly flays them alive, stripping off their skin, piece by delicious piece.

If they somehow survive this frankly horrific experience, Black Annis then delights in disemboweling them before drinking all their blood and feasting on their still-steaming intestines! Sweet!

Afterward, she decorates the walls of her cave with the leftover skin. Once the skin has turned to leather, Black Annis proudly wears it around her waist as a skirt, strutting up and down like a fashion model on the catwalk!

Case Study 043/9BA

Black Annis's Bower was described in the nineteenth century as being a mere four to five feet wide and seven to eight feet long, with stone ledges running along each side.

The British Cave Rescue Guild (BCRG), whose members help rescue people lost or trapped in the many caves of Britain, runs its own website. Here are two reports about emergency calls out to Black Annis's Bower.

WEDNESDAY 20 MARCH at 1425

(for three hours and forty-five minutes) (seventeen team members)

A twenty-seven-year-old registered "monster hunter" fell down a crevice while investigating the infamous Black Annis's Bower, and became tightly jammed between rocks. Numerous attempts to pull him free ended in failure because the rope mysteriously broke each time.

It is believed that the buildup of carbon dioxide (CO_2) from his own respiration caused this man to lose consciousness, and when finally hauled to the surface almost four hours later, he was already dead by asphyxiation.

POSTSCRIPT: Original diagnosis of death may have been wrong. A postmortem reveals that the man's larynx was literally crushed by an incredible force, almost as if an iron hand had squeezed tightly around it.

FRIDAY 10 MAY at 1115

(for two days) (forty-six team members)

Emergency call to all team members in the search for a missing female child, eleven years of age, last seen talking to an old woman around the vicinity of Black Annis's Bower. Believing that the child may have inadvertently wandered into the cave and become disoriented and lost in its dark underbelly, rescuers were ordered to the scene.

On the second day, the child's favorite bracelet was discovered, giving rescuers hope that she would be found alive. Entering a tunnel, rescuers were horrified to find strips of human skin hanging from the walls as well as a huge pile of human and animal bones piled up in a corner. Police were called in, and the investigation handed over to them. The child was never found and the rescue effort was called off.

BLACK ANNIS FACT FILE

Location: The county of Leicestershire, England
Appearance: Crinkly crone with blue skin, iron claws, and five sets of teeth
Strength: She can carry away human adults, so rather sinewy for her age
Weaknesses: The sun will turn her to stone!
Powers: Shape-shifter. Possible immortality. Magic.
Fear Factor: 69.3

HOW TO DESTROY BLACK ANNIS

Set up large mirrors all around the entrance to Black Annis's Bower. This will reflect bright sunlight inside the cave, turning Black Annis to stone!

OF BIPEDS OR TWO FOOTED BEASTS.

THE CYNOCEPHALUS

"Dog-Man of Andaman, feral and proud,
To his enemies, death, no compassion allow'd;
Dining on flesh bloodied and foul,
The air rent asunder by his victorious howl."

From a witch who can shape-shift into a cat, to a race of humans with the head of a dog!

Canine note: All dogs are descended from a small weasel-like mammal scientists have tagged *Miacis* (say me-ASS-iss), which appeared around forty million years ago during the Eocene Epoch. (The Eocene Epoch is split into the Early, Middle, and Late Eocene Epoch, and lasted from approximately 56–33.9 million years ago.)

Cynocephali (the plural form) are a warrior-like race that has been around at least four thousand years. Petroglyphs (rock carvings) dating from this period have been discovered on cliffs and boulders in the deserts of western Libya depicting dog-headed men hunting rhino.

Depending on whom you ask, these Freaky Fidos are either bloodthirsty barbarians who delight in the hunt, or else they're extremely civilized creatures who excel at farming, basket-weaving, raft-building, dressmaking, and growing spices.

Originating from the Andaman Islands (the 572 Andaman Islands are situated in the Bay of Bengal in the Indian Ocean), the Cynocephali were soon expanding their range to China, North Africa, and Europe.

Described as enormously tall with a mastiff's head, dark skin, large teeth, sharp claws, and a long tail, the Cynocephali also breathe fire and live for at least 170 to 200 years!

Benedictine monk Paul the Deacon (ca. AD 720s–799) wrote in his six-book opus *Historia gentis Langobardorum* that the Cynocephali "wage war obstinately, drink human blood, and quaff their own gore if they cannot reach the foe."

And Italian explorer and trader Marco Polo (ca. 1254–1324) stopped at Andaman Island for a quick bathroom break during his twenty-four-year journey around Asia with his pa and uncle. (Travel note: They departed Venice in 1271 when Marco was seventeen and didn't return until 1295, having traveled fifteen thousand miles!)

Meeting with Cynocephali while watering the flowers, Marco later revealed in the pages of his best-selling travelogue *Livre des merveilles du monde* (*Book of the Marvels of the World*; English title: *The Travels of Marco Polo*, published ca. 1300) that "They are a most cruel generation, and eat everybody that they can catch, if not of their own race."

Jesus of Nazareth, the dude who introduced Christianity to the masses, had a run-in with a Cynocephali in the form of one of his own followers, the later-to-be Saint Christopher, patron saint of travelers.

Reports claim that Ol' Chris was a large man with a dog's head. He was a wild and fierce warrior who came from a tribe of savage dog-headed men.

Luckily, Jesus had recently been to dog-training school, and soon taught Chris to sit, roll over, and play dead!

Repenting his warrior past, Chris became baptized and later received sainthood, and was gifted with human appearance!

Case File 663/12C

This book series and a kazillion others would not exist if not for two ultracool eighteenth-century English dudes who decided that kids were as entitled to read books as were adults, and put their money where their mouths were.

The first was publisher John Newbery (1713-1767), called "the Father of Children's Literature," for publishing some of the very first books aimed specifically at children!

The other was writer and publisher Thomas Boreman, of whom very little is known except that he produced a number of kid-friendly titles.

It was Thomas who wrote the incredibly popular kids' book *A Compendium of Zoology: Being A Description of More than Three Hundred Animals.*

First published in 1730, this natural-history book listed various animals and cryptids of all descriptions.

During our investigations, we uncovered a chapter on the Cynocephali that Thomas accidentally left out of the book!

BOOK 5
OF BIPEDS OR TWO-FOOTED BEASTS.
THE CYNOCEPHALUS.

"Dog-Man of Andaman, feral and proud,
To his enemies, death, no compassion allow'd;
Dining on flesh bloodied and foul,
The air rent asunder by his victorious howl."

The Cynocephalus, justly recognized as *the Warrior beast*, is part man, part canid. Its large, square dog's head is generally of a swarthy coloration; the small, V-shaped ears are dark; the muzzle half the length of the skull; the teeth pointed and sharp; the eyes, set wide apart, are of a brown or dark hazel hue; its fingernails like those of other animals except longer and rounder; both men and women have long and hairy tails set high, thick at the base, and tapering to a point.

The human physiology of this creature is exemplified by its muscular physique. At a most young age, a Cynocephalus cub is daily trained in the masterly art of hunting; upon the cusp of adulthood, he is sent out to make his first kill: Swift of foot, he does chase after prey and soon overcomes it. His strength is so impressive that he carries off a full-grown bull, like an eagle does a field mouse.

We read, also, in an author of great eminence, the Greek physician and historian Ctesias, writing around 400 BC, that the Cynocephali dwell not in houses like humans, but in mountain caves as far as the river Indus. The women bathe once monthly, the men not at all, except for their hands; and all anoint themselves with mink oil and dry themselves with animal skins.

CYNOCEPHALUS FACT FILE

Location: Asia, North Africa, Europe
Appearance: Dog-headed humanoids
Strength: Rabid
Weaknesses: Can't resist digging up flower beds, peeing up lampposts, and howling at the moon
Powers: Fire-breathers, long life
Fear Factor: 53

WHAT TO DO WITH A CAPTURED CYNOCEPHALUS

Enter it into a professional dog show as Best of Breed!

DISEMBOWELER

Case: 55'/63D

This female creepzoid really does exactly what it says on the label!

Set your smartphone's GPS (Global Positioning System) tracker to latitudes 59° and 83' N and longitudes 11° and 74' W and wrap up warm, because we're heading for Greenland!

The world's largest island, stretching approximately 830,000 square miles, about eighty percent of which is covered by a gargantuan ice sheet fourteen times the size of Louisiana or England, Greenland (aka *Kalaallit Nunaat* to the locals, of which there are approximately 57,000, give or take anyone accidentally being eaten by a passing walrus) is part of the continent of North America—although, just to confuse matters, Greenland is actually an autonomous country within the Kingdom of Denmark! Twisted!

Anyhow, these nice Inuit folk who make up eighty-nine percent of Greenland's populace are having big problems with the fiendishly frenzied and seemingly immortal Late Night Creature Feature known as . . . the Disemboweler!

The origins of Dissy (as we like to call her) are lost in Greenland's icy mists of myths and legends.

Apparently, Inuit shamans, during their intense mystical rituals, believed that they took a trip to "the land on top of the sky" to pay a house call on the gods Brother Moon and Sister Sun.

But first they had to pass by a grotesque being known as the Disemboweler.

Aside from her usual hag-type features and long, straggly hair, she had a retch-inducing deep hollow in her back, allowing one to see straight through into her spine! Bleh!

Well, Dissy was (and still is!) kind of evil, and tried to delay the shamans by making them laugh with her outrageous nonsensical dancing and gurning (making silly faces). And most of them did laugh. Whoops! Bad move, guys!

The moment a titter or guffaw sprang from their lips, Dissy would whip out her ulo (Eskimo for a woman's knife) and take delicious pleasure in . . . gutting them alive!

Now understandably, the moon and sun gods were a bit peeved by the remains of disemboweled shamans cluttering up the place, and so banished Dissy to Greenland, where she has continued her bonkers reign of terror ever since!

And she's slightly improved on her MO (modus operandi—Latin for "method of operation").

Not only does she waylay and chow down on any lonely Inuk (the singular noun of Inuit) traveling at night through the wilderness; she also sneaks into villages and whispers truly awful jokes to people, making them laugh so hard that their stomachs burst open from within!

So if you're a natural giggler—watch out!

Case Study 557/63D

The following report was obtained under the Freedom of Information Act. It was filed by an agent of the Central Bureau of Investigation, the clandestine American government agency that investigates all paranormal sightings. Dates, names, and specific locations have been redacted to protect the innocent.

Rock Hardy
CBI Special Agent
Case No.: 693/88/04D_____
Greenland
████████ January 19 ████

    This agent has been sent to the small town of ████████ in Greenland on what he suspects is yet another wild goose chase. It seems some kooky old dame is bumping off the locals. The Inuit leader ████████████ claims it is a supernatural witch-woman called the Disemboweler. Yeah, right.

In freezing temperatures, which this agent has been trained not to feel, he begins his patrol on the outskirts of ████████.

One full hour and thirteen minutes pass by, and then this agent notices the shriveled figure of a crinkly old woman tramping through the deep snow toward him. In one hand she carries a sharp-bladed flat knife!

Immediately, this agent reaches for his standard issue Glock 23 semi-automatic and aims it at her head. "Drop the weapon, sister!" he commands. "Or I'll plug you where you stand!"

"But dearie," she cackles insanely. "I just want to tell you some jokes! Trust me! You'll burst out laughing! Heeheeheeeee!"

This agent doesn't want to offend the ole gal——it's useful to keep the locals on one's side——and she seems harmless enough, so he gives her the affirmative to continue.

She tells this agent one joke. And another. And then another. But CBI agents have absolutely no sense of humor. When this agent doesn't even twitch a lip, the dame suddenly turns ugly. She throws herself at him, knife poised to strike!

Expertly dodging the attack, this agent's foot slips in the snow and he crashes to the ground, dropping his weapon!

Expecting death by blade at any moment, he sees a blur of white swiftly pass him by, followed by a high-pitched scream. Looking up, this agent watches a hungry polar bear rushing across the ████████████████, chasing after the maniacal madam.

Ursus maritimus, to give the furry mammal its scientific name, was later found gutted and half-eaten. Of the batty broad, there was no sign.

As per agreement with Regional Supervisor ████████████, this agent respectfully suggests that this case be closed, and not be presented to the relevant authorities on paranormal activities.

THE DISEMBOWELER FACT FILE

Location: Greenland
Appearance: Hideous hag with deep hole in her back
Strength: Fueled by madness, this lady packs a wallop!
Weaknesses: Pinch yourself to stop laughing, and she can't touch you
Powers: Probable immortality. A wiz with the ulo. Death jokes.
Fear Factor: For Inuit folk, 94.9

BEST USE OF THE DISEMBOWELER

Enter her into the World's Gurning Championships——she'll win hands down, and you'll collect the prize money!

And here's another *teramorphous* (abnormal or monstrous) therianthrope to add to your collection!

Pronounced Way CHEE bo, the name originates from both old Yucatán Maya (*Huay* meaning "sorcerer") and Spanish (*chivo* means "male goat"), and perfectly describes these flaky Central American shamans who sell their souls to the skeletal Mayan death god, Kisin, in exchange for the powers of black magic! (As you do!)

Cultural note: The Mayan civilization was one of the oldest and longest-surviving, located in what is now southern Mexico, Guatemala, Belize, western Honduras, and extreme northern El Salvador. It is cloaked in mystery, both as to when it first appeared and why it eventually disappeared.

Although Mayan artifacts have been unearthed in the ancient farming village of Cuello in Belize, and carbon-dated to at least 2600 BC, the currently accepted view by archaeologists (so guaranteed to be wrong!) is that the first proper Mayan settlement appeared "around" 1800 BC. *Whateverrrr,* it was a long time ago!

What is known is that these guys rocked when it came to being geniuses.

They developed two different (yet both perfect) calendar systems, one of the first (hieroglyphic) writing systems (they even published their own books!), a mathematical system, an increased knowledge of astronomy, a working system of government, agriculture (farming), weaving and fine pottery, art, amazing temples, amazing pyramids and sprawling cities, road systems, aqueducts and underground reservoirs (in the jungle, no less!), extensive trade routes with other civilizations, ball games, corn tortillas, and . . . chocolate! (Anyone who thought up chocolate gets our vote!)

The Mayan civilization reached its peak in AD 600, but most of the cities were mysteriously abandoned by AD 900. Scholars are still stumped as to why. The civilization finally disappeared for good after the Spanish invasions and wholesale slaughter of the indigenous populace in the sixteenth century. (Well, that would do it!)

Anyway, getting back to our mad monks, to seal the pact with the bone-rattling satanic deity Kisin, the shamans get together for afternoon tea and cucumber sandwiches.

Afterward, they stand in a circle of lighted black candles holding hands (aww, sweet!), reciting the Lord's Prayer backward nine times before cutting the throat of a poor, defenseless young goat and glugging down its thick, warm blood!

But ol' Kisin, he speaketh with forked tongue, and while he does indeed grant these depraved loons everything they wish for, he also curses them horribly, forevermore transforming their human heads into goats' heads with glowing red eyes!

(You can just imagine the scene when a shaman returns home after said ritual!):

Not that these shamans complain too much. They now possess demonic dark powers, including the ability to shape-shift into any animal—goat, jaguar, deer, or their favorite form, a hideous huge black hellhound called Huay Perro (sorcerer-dog)!

Case Study 337/HC

Many a greedy, land-grabbing, warmongering, genocidal imperialistic country's leaders get their kicks outta invading other people's land and claiming it for themselves, brutally slaughtering untold numbers of innocent native inhabitants in the process, and the sixteenth-century Spanish were no exception.

Unfortunately for the conquistadores, the Mayans didn't go quietly, and it took 170 years of bloody fighting until the last city fell in 1697.

We have recently unearthed an ancient scroll written by an unnamed Mayan priest, describing an attack by the conquistadores on the coastal city of Tulum (aka Zama) in the Yucatán Peninsula in 1528. (Yeah, yeah, we've translated it for you!)

As foretold by the spilled blood of the sacrificial lamb upon this very morn, the invaders come once more to capture our city of Zama, called also the City of Dawn, for it faces the sunrise.

They come in hundreds, armed with spears and swords and long metal tubes that spit thunder! When this terrible weapon roars, a citizen falls, a strange hole appearing in head or chest. They are the weapons of the gods!

Thankfully, we have our own defense against such supernatural powers.

Our priests have called upon the death god, Kisin, to help us in our hour of need! The ritual over, their human heads transform into that of the sacred goat, their bodies imbued with dark eldritch magic!

With the sleeping of the sun, our priests set out along the dark jungle trails toward the enemy camp.

Our hearts sing with joy upon listening to the hideous death screams of the invaders. This lasts until the light of a new day dawns brightly.

When the goat-priests return, their mouths drip fresh blood. Only a few invaders escape, their uniforms in tatters, to warn their leaders to stay away.

(History note: The city of Tulum finally fell around the end of the sixteenth century, its demise the result of Old World [European] diseases the conquistadores brought with them, and for which the Mayans had no known cure.)

HUAY CHIVO FACT FILE

Location: The Mexican states of Yucatán, Campeche, and Quintana Roo
Appearance: Goat-headed man with glowing red eyes
Strength: Demonic god-fueled, so kind of tough!
Weaknesses: A really powerful book of spells might help fight off his evil magic—but don't quote us on that!
Powers: Black magic, hypnotism, therianthropy
Fear Factor: 92.1

BEST USE FOR A CAPTURED HUAY CHIVO

Goats eat anything and everything, so feed him all your nonrecyclable trash and help to save the planet! (And any resultant pile of goat's poo can be sold to gardeners to fertilize their roses! A win-win situation, and mondo profitable!)

KOSCHEI THE DEATHLESS

With a mondo chilling moniker like that, you just known this creep's going to be seriously hardcore to the max! (Trust us—he is!)

Kidnapper, sadist (a twisted soul who enjoys inflicting pain upon others), and all-around bloody murderer, Koschei the Deathless (aka Koschei the Immortal) is the Numero Uno supernatural terror in Slavic countries, most especially Russia, Poland, Ukraine, and the Czech Republic.

No surprise then (and kind of obvious by his handle) that not only is Koschei an all-powerful sorcerer, but—the freak cannot die! Ever!

(Well, there is *one* way to kill him, but it's so convoluted you'll probably die of old age yourself before you achieve it!)

Self-styled czar (from the Latin *Caesar*, meaning *"emperor"*), his name derives from the Slavic word *kost* ("bone"), which is rather apt since Koschei the Deathless is mostly eyeballed as a hideously emaciated or skeletal figure with barf-inducing extended arms and legs.

Stylishly sporting an unkempt mane of gray hair and a grungy beard, a naked Koschei rides his talking horse (a present from that Russian witch Baba Yaga) across the frozen steppes, brandishing a bloodstained saber and in search of young women, preferably the wife of a hero, to kidnap, torture, and kill!

Something of an emo, if Koschei's prey escapes his bony clutches, he'll sit for hours, wailing and sobbing with frustrated rage, his anguished cries echoing through the Caucasus.

The reason for Koschei's immortality is his detachable soul, which he keeps (deep breath!) inside the point of a needle inside a duck's egg inside a rabbit or hare inside an iron or crystal box buried under a green oak tree inside a forest somewhere on a small island in an unspecified ocean on the other side of the world!

And the only way to defeat Koschei is to find said egg—and smash it against his forehead! (Told you it was complicated!)

Case Study 002/6KTD

In 1536, tyrannical psycho nutjob Henry VIII, king of England, Wales, and Ireland (1491–1547), had a big problem with the corrupt and rotten Roman Catholic Church. (Anyone who disagreed with the church was labeled a heretic and burned at the stake! Nice!)

Pope Clement VII (1478–1534) refused Henry permission to divorce Catherine of Aragon (1485–1536) and marry Anne Boleyn (ca.1507–1536).

Henry's answer? Disband the Catholic Church in England and establish the Church of England in its place—and guess who made up the new rules?! Ha! (Ya gotta love a despot!)

To escape persecution, many friars and monks thumbed a lift seaward and headed for pastures new.

One of this band of not-so-merry men was Franciscan monk Brother Jacob, who traveled the world bringing the word of God to those who would listen.

During this time, he also did bloodily smite a hideous monster or two!

Jacob kept a detailed record of these titanic struggles—including one against that foul, undying fiend, Koschei the Deathless!

THE ADVENTURES OF BROTHER JACOB

"God's teeth!" I did most fervently cry. "Thy rank pustule-blossom'd countenance blights even this curs'd earth!"

Upon a frozen wasteland stood I, the numbing Siberian winds howling around me like Satan's banshees burning within the fiery Bowels of Hell and Damnation!

Barring my path, a sight of foul degradation! Its pestilential visage did all but scour my eyes blind with unholy terror!

Blaspheming the Heavenly Father by his shocking nakedness of form stood the skeletal deformity known by simple Slavic peoples as Koschei the Deathless—his name alone an abomination in the eyes of his Holiness the All-Knowing, who grants all sweet death so that they may ascend heavenward!

"Foolish mortal!" hissed this purveyor of wickedness. "Stand aside—or die!"

"The village yonder has requested my aid in ridding them of your fetid presence, you Mephistophelian Monstrosity!" replied I, raising my sacred sword, Seraph. "And as God's one true agent on earth, I make good on my promises!"

With the guiding hand of the Infinite Spirit upon my shoulder, I leaped to smite my foe!

And sailed straight through him as the damnable shape-changer's body turned to mist!

His body whipping around in a frenetic Apollyon-gifted whirlwind, Beelzebub's beast bore down upon me!

"Die, mortal!" he cackled, the elongated arms reaching out and wrapping tightly around my head to snap my neck! *"Diiiiiiie!"*

Smiling triumphantly, I pulled forth from my cassock's pocket a large duck's egg.

"Before the spiritual sojourn that brought me here, the king of kings sent his loyal soldier to a small island on the other side of the world!" I exclaimed with biblical fervor. "And now, foul fiend——Judgment Day be upon thee!"

"Noooo! Give that back!" lamented that evil incarnate——too late! The egg smashed upon his cankerous forehead!

Gleefully watching the demon instantaneously vanish back to his rightful place in Hades, I exalted, "Thou hast sown the wind! And must now reap the whirlwind! Praise be the Lord!"

Hallelujah!

KOSCHEI THE DEATHLESS FACT FILE

Location: Slavic countries
Appearance: Tall, hairy, naked, skeletal dude with talking horse!
Strength: Hellish!
Weaknesses: The breaking of his soul egg!
Powers: Sorcery. Transmogrification. Weather control. Venomous bite. Immortality.
Fear Factor: 99.9

HOW TO KILL KOSCHEI THE DEATHLESS

Locate the soul egg. Invite Koschei to breakfast and serve him the egg boiled. Koschei will eat his own soul and revert back to the living, allowing you to use his own saber to——chop off his head! Poetic justice! Sweet!

QUIGLEY'S TRUTH

CTESIAS WAS A GREEK PHYSICIAN TO THE PERSIAN RULER ARTAXERXES II MNEMON IN THE EARLY FIFTH CENTURY, BC.

ON 3RD SEPTEMBER 401 BC, HE ACCOMPANIED THE KING TO WAGE WAR AGAINST ARTAXERXES'S TRAITOROUS YOUNGER BROTHER CYRUS THE YOUNGER!

THE BATTLE OF CUNAXA TOOK PLACE 44 MILES NORTH OF BABYLON, THE 44,520 SOLDIERS OF CYRUS AGAINST ARTAXERXES'S ARMY OF 40,000!

DURING THE BLOODY SKIRMISH, IT IS CLAIMED THAT CTESIAS GLIMPSED A MONSTROUS SIGHT!

BY THE GODS! WHAT IS – THAT?!

GRRROOOWWWL!

STORY CONTINU

Ooo-kaaay! This one's a bit tricky! The manticore is a deadly vicious man-monster that definitely needs hunting down—and yet if you catch but a glimpse of this hellacious human-snacking horror, you've already snuffed it! (Shucks!)

Not that it possesses a wackadoodle-cool death-stare power or anything, but once it catches your scent it won't stop tracking ya, no matter where you run!

A *chimera* (a creature made up from various animal parts), the Manticore has the double-sized body of a lion, bloodred fur, a human head, blue or gray eyes, three rows of shark-sharp teeth (most actual sharks have *five* rows of teeth, numbering up to three thousand! Imagine brushing those three times a day!), and a scorpion's stinger or dragon-style tail that fires off poisonous spines! (He can also walk upright if he fancies!)

Some even possess wings but can't fly, although the Manticore's prodigious leaps make up for that lil' failing!

And if that isn't enough, Manny also has a hypnotic melodious human speaking voice, much like the haunting mixture of panpipes and trumpet that he uses to lure his victims into his clutches!

Unlike his kooky cousin the sphinx, who feeds on females, the Manticore prefers crunching down on the bones of men and boys. And he's no wuss! He'll gladly attack two or three adults at one time, and kills them all! Every time!

Taught by his dear ol' mom (yeah, his mom! Where'd you *think* he came from? The stork?! Sheesh!) not to waste food, Manny gulps down everything of his prey, including the buttons on the bloodied clothes!

First appearing in the ancient kingdom of Persia, where he was named *Martyaxwar*— literally *martya* ("man" or "human") and *xwar* ("to eat")—the Manticore soon spread west, where he was known to the ancient Greeks as *Martichora* and later to the Romans (thanks to a typo by not-so-clever-clogs Pliny the Elder, who was foolishly tricked by the spelling demon Titivillus!) as *Manticorus*.

Nowadays, the Manticore is mostly spotted prowling the lush forests of India, although there have been reports from as far afield as Spain and North America!

Almost invincible to any form of weapon or magic, the Manticore does have one major weakness: natural light! Both daylight and moonlight will shrivel him into ash! So, as long as you don't go a-hunting him in the dark, you should be fine! (Fingers crossed!)

Case Study 331/44M

Robert LeRoy Ripley (1890–1949) was an American cartoonist, entrepreneur (savvy businessman!), and amateur anthropologist who, like us, loved digging up amazing true facts about this kooky world we live in. (Respect!)

His Ripley's Believe It or Not! brand has developed into books, TV series, radio shows, comic books, museums, and theme parks worldwide.

It all started with a daily newspaper strip called *Champs and Chumps*, which first appeared on December 19, 1918, celebrating great sporting achievements. In October 1919, the strip changed both its focus and its title to the one so loved today!

There have been many copycat series, including the less-successful *Quigley's Truth Or Fiction?!* Only one page of *Quigley's* comic strip—about the Manticore, no less!—has survived, which we've reprinted at the start of this chapter.

The rest of the story continues here in comic strip script form!

PAGE 2

Panel I

CAP: HIS MIND WHIRLING, CTESIAS FAILED TO NOTICE AN ENEMY SOLDIER ATTACKING——UNTIL IT WAS TOO LATE!

One of Cyrus's soldiers raises a sword to strike down the defenseless Ctesias.

SOLDIER: DIE, FOLLOWER OF ARTAXERXES! *DIIIIE!*

CTESIAS: *AAAAAHHHH!*

Panel 2

CAP: IN AN EFFORT TO EVADE CERTAIN DEATH, CTESIAS STUMBLED! JUST AS THE STRANGE CREATURE——LEAPED!

Ctesias is stumbling backward, out of the path of the swinging sword. The Manticore leaps toward the combatants.

CTESIAS: *YAAAH!*

MANTICORE: *RRRRRH!*

Panel 3

CAP: THE MONSTER'S MOUTH OPENED WIDE AND SWALLOWED THE SOLDIER——*WHOLE*!
The Manticore's huge mouth is open wide, swallowing the soldier inside of it.

SOLDIER: NYAAAAAAGGGGH!

SFX: CHOMP!

Panel 4

CAP: ITS HUNGER SATIATED, THE MONSTER DEPARTED!
Ctesias watches in amazement as the Manticore runs off across the plain.

CTESIAS: BLESSED BE! IT IS A *MARTICHORA*—A MAN-EATER!

Panel 5

CAP: CYRUS WAS KILLED IN BATTLE AND ARTAXERXES KEPT HIS THRONE UNTIL HE DIED IN EITHER 359 OR 358 BC.

Large panel. Ctesias and Artaxerxes stand on a balcony of the royal palace, looking out across the glory that is the kingdom of Persia. In the sky above, we can see a red storm cloud in the image of the Manticore.

CAP (bottom of page): CTESIAS LATER WROTE OF SEEING THE MONSTER AGAIN DURING HIS TRAVELS IN INDIA. HE WAS THE FIRST TO COIN THE TERM *MARTICHORA*—MANTICORE! TRUTH OR FICTION? *YOU* DECIDE!

THE END

(Any budding artist who fancies drawing this strip, knock yourself out!)

MANTICORE FACT FILE

Location: Forests of the continent of Asia, especially India, Indonesia, and Malaysia; the Middle East, Europe, North America
Appearance: Lion-man!
Strength: Horrifying!
Weaknesses: Natural light (wimpo!)
Powers: Hypnotism. Bad luck and misfortune—well, it is if you run into one!
Fear Factor: Daytime/moonlight—a big fat zero! Total darkness—93.7

COOL USE FOR THE MANTICORE

Use its scorpion stinger as a bottle opener——your parties will be the talk of the neighborhood!

November – 23rd

NUCKELAVEE

In our amped-up _Monster Hunters Unlimited_ series, we've brought you some truly _barf-_inducing monsters.

But none with such monumental _barfness_ as Nuckelavee, the totally flayed hybrid man-Horse!

The founder of the Chinese Ming Dynasty Emperor Zhu Yuanzhang (1328–1398) got such a kick outta the spectacle that in 1396, he ordered five thousand terrified women to be flayed alive for his entertainment! (There being nothing much on TV that night!)

There're no words gross enough to describe this heart attack city mugly-bugly!

For starters, as so eloquently described by Gibraltar-born Scottish writer, poet, and baronet Sir George Brisbane Scott Douglas (1856–1935) in his book _The Scottish Antiquary_

(1891): "The whole surface of the monster appeared like raw and living flesh, from which the skin had been stripped. You could see the black blood flowing through his veins, and every movement of his muscles, when the horrid creature moved, showed white sinews in motion."

Its horse's head (some say elongated "human" head) is ten times bigger than a normal man's, with one large single eye that burns with a fiery flame. And a ginormous mouth that resembles a pig's snout and that can swallow a human whole!

Razor-sharp fins grow up its four legs, and from out of its back grows the hideous, distorted, and legless torso of a man whose arms are so long they almost drag along the ground!

The head on top of the torso is so large the neck cannot hold the weight, causing the head to loll back and forth, threatening to fall off!

Hailing from the wild heather of the Orkney Islands in Scotland (the Orkneys are made up of around seventy small islands, only twenty of which are inhabited and have been for at least the past 8,500 years), the demonic Nuckelavee is the most evil and degenerate of all Unseelie fairies.

Rising up from its home beneath the turbulent seas around the Orkneys (considered to be some of the most dangerous seas on the planet), the Nuckelavee goes on a horrifying rampage across the islands!

Its fetid breath brings about deadly disease in both humans and animals, blights crops, and creates ruinous drought!

He also gets his kicks outta dragging unwary humans into the sea to feast on their succulent flesh!

HUNDA.

Case Study 588/39N

Fifteen-year-old Soul-Gon McDonald of Wollongong, New South Wales, has kindly allowed us to reproduce one of the entries in her monster-hunter diary.

November 23

G'day, diary!

Da oldies have dragged me from a heat-scorchin' summer in Oz with me mates for a blow in to the frozen hell that is Scotland in winter. Yaay.

They wanted a gander at where me true-blue great-great-whatever gramps lived before getting sent on a convict ship down under!

I was spittin' th' dummy about being here until I heard tell of recent sightings of a Fred Nerk on one of th' uninhabited Orks!

Being a stickybeak, I said "ta ta" t' th' oldies f' th' day, 'n' went Waltzin' Matilda on a bus to Burray 'n' then across a causeway to th' island o' Hunda for a squiz on me pat.

Strewth, what a dump! Aside from a few sheep and goats 'n' a kazillion seabirds, there was Sweet Fanny Adams. An hour of sidestepping bird poo 'n' I was right ticked.

Then I smelt something seriously iffy! Someone—or something—had just let off an almighty fluff! Man, did it hum!

Turning, I saw a hideous fusion o' bloodred half-man half-horse! The creature had a face like a robber's dog 'n' an all-over Dad 'n' Dave, so close that he was completely skinned! Ewww! Gross!

"Orright?" I asked, feeling a little toey 'cos I knew a Nuckelavee when I googled one.

Movin' toward me, the monster's single eye blazed with unearthly hatred! Remembering stories of his deadly halitosis, I slowly reached down for me Aristotle, unscrewing the lid.

As it made ready to huff 'n' puff over me, I grinned. "Rack off, ya nong!" I shouted, throwing the contents o' pure Scottish spring water in its face.

There was an almighty screech and Nuncky tore arse before leaping into the sea 'n' disappearing! Bonzer! Hooroo!

G'day: Hello

Oldies: Parents

Oz: Australia

Blow in: unexpected visit

Gander: a good look

True-blue: genuine

Down Under: Australia

Spitting the dummy: very angry

Fred Nerk: imaginary creature

Orks: Orkney Islands

Stickybeak: a nosy person

Ta ta (pronounced "tati-tah"): good-bye

Waltzing Matilda: wandering (waltzing) with your gear wrapped in a blanket or sleeping bag (Matilda)

Squiz: quick look

Pat: alone

Strewth: exclamation of surprise

Sweet Fanny Adams: nothing

Ticked: annoyed

Fluff: fart

Hum: stink

Face like a robber's dog: seriously ugly

Dad 'n' Dave: shave

Orright: all right (a greeting, like "Hello")

Toey: anxious, nervous

Aristotle: bottle

Rack off!: scram!

Nong: idiot

To tear arse: to run away very fast

Bonzer: great

Hooroo: Good-bye

NUCKELAVEE FACT FILE

Location: The Orkney Islands, Scotland

Appearance: Pulsating red raw flesh-flayed horse-man combo!

Strength: Satanic!

Weaknesses: Fresh water—hates the stuff

Powers: The 3 Ds—drought, disease, and death!

Fear Factor: For Orcadians (people from Orkney)—82.9. The rest of us? Pfft!

WHAT TO DO WITH A CAPTURED NUCKELAVEE

Enter him into the UK's famous Grand National horse race. His hideous form will scare off all the other horses and you'll win by default! Easy!

Fee-fi-fo-fum,
I smell the blood of an Englishman,
Be he live, or be he dead,
I'll grind his bones to make my bread.

You must have heard this ditty before! It's the most famous and well-known quatrain (a four-line poem or stanza) in the fairy-tale biz!

   (Musical note: A *stanza* is a verse within a longer poem or song. Not to be confused, of course, with the *refrain*, or the "chorus." A *couplet*, by the way, is a two-line verse.)

   "Hold on!" we hear you aggressively yell. "What's a stanza from *Jack and the Beanstalk*, a fairy tale about a *giant*, gotta do with ogres?! Aren't they different?"

Glad you asked!

This sickly dank fairy story is believed to have started as a creepy oral story from those *uber*cool manic warriors, the Norse Vikings (*vikingr* in Old Norse dialect), whose blood-spilling raiding parties scared the sweet bejeebers out of many a helpless villager across Europe between the late eighth and mid-eleventh centuries.

Back then, and right up to 1890 when Australian historian, literary critic, and folklorist (dude who studies folklore) Joseph Jacobs (1854–1916) rewrote this classic for a new generation, the Castle-in-the-Sky owner was . . . an *ogre*!

It was only in later recordings that the evil ogre changed into a giant!

An aside: How come the ogre/giant is considered the villain of the piece? Someone breaks into his home, steals his belongings and murders him, and *he's* the bad guy?! If kids are spoon-fed this type of "moral" tripe while growing up, no wonder humans turn out the way they do!

Ogres have been around since before the Neanderthals (ca. 200,000 to 30,000 years ago, and close cousins to us bunch, *Homo sapiens*) first figured out that it's best not to stick a sharp, pointy stick up the nose to scrape out the boogers.

Appearing worldwide, this man-monster's handle first appeared in print (as far as anyone knows) around 1181–1191 in poet and troubadour (composer and performer) Chrétien de Troyes's cracking romance poem "Perceval, ou Le Conte du Graal" ("Percerval, the Story of the Grail").

Others argue that the word was created by other French (and even Italian) writers.

A tad shorter than giants, these superhuman ogres are brutish with a seriously low IQ, (intelligence quotient). They have large heads; hairy, muscle-pumping bodies; and huge bellies, which comes from eating humans whole, their favorite dessert being wailing tots. (And they're gladly welcome to them, we say!)

Preferring a solitary life in the forests and mountains, ogres simply want to be left in peace. Shame then that there are seven billion–plus destructive humans on this planet to mess up that little life's dream! Hey ho!

Case Study 659/720

Any American wrestling fans out there? Well, we hate to burst your bubble, bub, but the wrestling ISN'T real. It's all pretend, dude! You know—FAKE! The "wrestlers" (actors) are given a script to follow during each match, the outcome preordained.

For some bizarre reason, millions of people worldwide love watching this nonsense. Sad.

However, occasionally *real* wrestling matches are held. One recent bout of savage fury saw the Myth Wrestling Federation's reigning champion the Ogre face off against the number-one contender—Jack the Beanstalk! And here's a transcript of the action!

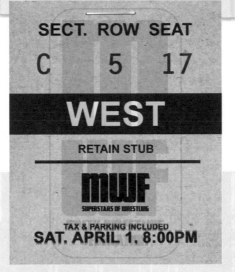

SECT. ROW SEAT

C   5   17

WEST

RETAIN STUB

mWF
SUPERSTARS OF WRESTLING

TAX & PARKING INCLUDED
SAT. APRIL 1, 8:00PM

BATTLE OF THE MILLENNIUM!
THE OGRE vs. JACK the BEANSTALK!

The show everyone's been waiting for is finally here! The grudge match of the century! One will live! One will die! And one will be crowned—the Titan of Titans!

There he is, folks! The challenger, Jack the Beanstalk, has stepped into the ring, flexing his puny muscles to the excited roar of the human crowd! We don't need to guess who they're supporting!

And here's the world's tallest athlete! Topping fifty feet and twelve thousand pounds, the Ogre is one angry dude, with a mega mean-on toward the Beanstalk for daring to challenge his undefeated status!

With one stride, the Ogre steps into the ring, his huge feet filling the canvas! The two combatants snarl threateningly, psyching each other out!

Is the Ogre invincible . . . or is tonight the night that there's a new king in town?!

The bell rings! The first man to gain pinfall, submission, or count-out will win the Belt and be proclaimed champion!

The Beanstalk immediately leaps against the ropes, catapulting off to slam into the Ogre's leg! Oooh! No dice! All the fool's done is knock himself senseless!

Oh man! This doesn't look good! The Ogre is lifting up the Beanstalk by his foot and . . . he's stuffing the Beanstalk into his cavernous mouth, headfirst! *Ewww!* Gross!

Oooh! Just hear those bones snapping! And yep, Jack has lost his head—literally! The Ogre burps loudly, tossing aside the headless torso. Jack's only got a count of ten to get back into the ring!

Eight! Nine! And—it's all over!

The Ogre is once again supreme sovereign, and . . . oh no! Now he's scooping up handfuls of spectators and eating them!

And now he's heading our way! *Aaaaaaaah!*

Transcript ends.

OGRE FACT FILE

Location: Worldwide; ubershy, so although on the tall side, rather hard to spot!

Appearance: Gargantuan! (And smelly! Not known for personal hygiene! Man, those skid marks in the underwear! Stinkville! Aookk!!)

Strength: Weight-lifts small mountains!

Weaknesses: Fire. Acid. Pretty princesses in castles—ogres are seriously emo when it comes to falling in lurrve!

Powers: Superstrength

Fear Factor: They're not that scary! 26.4—if you're a wimp!

HOW TO CASH IN ON AN OGRE

Sell one of his sneakers to the Old Woman Who Lived in a Shoe as the latest in modern housing for her and her unruly brood!

Say a warm Indonesian "Selamat pagi!" ("Good morning!") and "Apa kabar?" ("How are you?") to this sanguivorous (blood-drinking) vampire-ghost who preys upon the unfortunate people of the tropical countries of Malaysia and Indonesia in Southeast Asia!

Travel note: Indonesia is an archipelago [a chain of islands] made up of 17,508 islands upon which live more than 238 million people, making it the world's fourth-largest country after the Republic of China [with a population of approximately 1.36 billion], India [1.23 billion], and the United States [318 million].

The Pontianak is the vengeful spirit of a young woman who has died while pregnant.

Having a huge dislike for humans, especially the male of the species, the Pontianak transforms herself into a stunningly beautiful woman dressed all in white, and with long hair and pale skin to entice foolish young men into her clutches.

Once close to her prey, she holds tight to the back of his head, whispering sweet nothings into his ear—before sharply stabbing her razor talons into his stomach and ripping out his steaming, bloodied intestines, which she ravenously devours! (Rapacious!)

And if you're foolish enough to stare longingly into her eyes as she's promising you your heart's fondest desires—she'll suck out your eyeballs and swallow them whole!

On occasion, if feeling particularly hungry, the Pontianak will gobble down any spare baby lying around.

If you want to stay clear of such a gross demise, we suggest following the example of those sensible Malay people and don't hang out your washing to dry overnight.

For in those sunset hours between dusk and dawn, the Pontianak will glide into the garden and hungrily sniff the clothes, reveling in the scent of her next victim!

There are two proven ways to recognize if a Pontianak is on your trail:

If you hear a baby wailing or a dog howling loudly, the Pontianak is far away. If they whimper quietly, she's on your doorstep!

When she's close, you'll first smell a sweet floral fragrance of Plumeria, which quickly turns into the puke-inducing stench of . . . death!

(Gardening note: Plumeria is a tropical shrub or tree with beautiful flowers from which floral garlands are made. Better known as Frangipani, it is a member of the dogbane family of flowering trees and shrubs.)

Best defense against a Pontianak? Carry a hammer and iron nail wherever you go! Sneak up behind her and drive the nail into the back of her neck! She'll immediately obey your every command! (But only so long as the nail stays in place! If it's removed, all bets are off!)

Case Study 119/52P

Be prepared to barf your breakfast when you hear this, but romance (we know—ick!) is Big Business!

Worldwide sales of romance novels top a mind-numbing two BILLION dollars—yes, two BILLION!!!—every year!

Although many people believe English writer Jane Austen (1775-1817) to be one of the original instigators of love pap with her novel *Sense and Sensibility* (published in 1811), the first romance novel was actually published more than seventy years before!

English writer and printer Samuel Richardson (1689-1761) wrote and published *Pamela: Or, Virtue Rewarded*, in 1740.

This is also one of the first fictional stories to be written as "diary entries," and, we would guess, one of the first-ever self-published books! (And not an e-reader in sight!)

For your entertainment and delight (c'mon, you know you want to!) we've unearthed a 1950s true romance short story about a man who fell in love with—the Pontianak!

THE FOOD OF LOVE

On the hot white sands of Kuta Beach, we lie entwined, dappled sunlight skimming across the rich, crystalline aqua-blue waves of the rolling Indian Ocean.

A gentle summer breeze and the hungry cry of a passing Streaked Shearwater the only disturbance to our tranquility.

"I-I love you, my sweetness," I whisper; my lips, wet with anticipation, lightly caressing a trembling earlobe.

"I-I do, too," comes the breathless reply, eyes sparkling with rapturous desire.

Gently sliding my fingernails across his bare stomach, I playfully push against the trickling sweat. My love giggles.

I push again, harder this time, and hear a surprised grunt of pleasure . . . or is it from a jolt of pain?

No matter, we are now as one, bound together. Smiling sweetly, I thrust my fingernails deeper still, splitting through the stomach lining.

Even deeper, reaching for the warm intestines I can feel palpitating excitedly inside of the body.

Flowing blood allows my fingers to glide smoothly around them. Violently ripping them free, a death-terror scream echoes from his lips.

Gurgling, unable to cry out, he stares up in disbelieving horror at his bloody bowels hanging loosely in my hand.

"But I love *feasting* on you, human, even more!" I cackle, leaning close to passionately suck out his eyeballs!

When I have finished, I glance down contemptuously at the dead creature before me.

"Oh well," I sigh. "Now I'm going to have to find myself *another* boyfriend!"

The End

PONTIANAK FACT FILE

Location: The banana trees of Malaysia, Indonesia, and the Philippines
Appearance: Disguises herself as a beautiful young woman—yeah, we know, not much help!
Strength: Vampiric
Weaknesses: A single nail. A sharp thorn.
Powers: Shape-shifter. Flight. Bloodsucker.
Fear Factor: 57

BADASSICAL USE FOR A PONTIANAK

Make her use her sharp talons to shred your poor school report card before your mom sees it— and then blame the mess on the neighbor's cat!

SPRING-HEELED JACK

Spring-Heeled Jack is an accipitral (predatory like a falcon) avatar of terror who attacked people across the United Kingdom with impunity (no one could stop him)—and what's even more shocking, he continues to appear, even today!

Described as a tall, gaunt man of "a devilish appearance," dressed in a dark cloak beneath which is a tight-fitting outfit similar to an oilskin, and oftentimes wearing a nightmare-inducing helmet, Jack's eyes are like "red balls of fire," and at the end of his clawed hands are metallic, razor-sharp fingertips!

His first recorded attack was in October 1837, when a young servant named Mary Stevens was accosted by a tall man with a powerful, superhuman grip! His fingers, she said, were "cold and clammy as those of a corpse!"

But Ol' Jack's most memorable party tricks were the ability to breathe out a pyrotechnic blue-and-white flame which could both momentarily blind his victims and cause them to suffer uncontrollable fits, and his amazing hopping-jumping ability that was on par with that Chinese undead vampire/zombie creepoid Jiang Shi!

According to witnesses, Jack's powerful leg muscles could propel him to heights of nine feet or more!

After attacking two young women in February 1838, he was seen escaping by making a standing jump from the ground to the roof of a house before bounding like a flea across rooftops, cackling with high-pitched laughter!

His favorite party tricks included leaping out of the darkness to slap someone across the cheek before bounding away; knocking on doors and scaring the inhabitants; and jumping in front of coaches, causing the startled driver to swerve and crash the vehicle! Bodacious!

Jack traveled the length of Britain throughout the nineteenth century, right up to 1904, when he made his last appearance in the northern city of Liverpool. And then—he disappeared!

And popped up in Louisville, Kentucky, where he was described as having pointy ears, a long nose and fingers, and emitting blue flames from—his chest!

Jack now spends his time "hopping" (excuse the pun!) back and forth between Britain and America (and occasionally stopping over in India!), raining down heart-stopping horror on his helpless victims!

Case Study 0057/18SHJ

Interest in supernatural and paranormal phenomena reached its height in Victorian Britain. Psychics and scientists alike investigated sightings of ghosts and monsters, demons and angels, dragons and fairies.

One of the leading lights of the movement was Lady Theodora Bennett, a beautiful and aristocratic philanthropist. (Translated from the Greek words *philein* and *anthropos*, philanthropy literally means "love of humanity"; usually a filthy-rich dude or dudette who uses his or her wealth to help others.)

Scientist, inventor, adventuress, and monster hunter, Theodora regularly traveled the world risking her life to discover the truth behind strange sightings and events.

Here is an address she made to The Royal Society of Monster Hunters members at their annual conference, regarding her encounter with Spring-Heeled Jack.

The
Royal Society
of
Monster Hunters
—
Established · 1764

December 15, 1838

My Lords, Ladies, and Men,

Soaring in good earnest like a hawk in search of prey, my airship, *The Grand Duchess*, crossed silently over the fogbound cityscape of Old London Town. Blasts of steam escaped with sprightly manner from the steam vents.

"Target located, ma'am," my demon familiar footman addressed me, adjusting his satin coat after hitherto pulling the necessary cranks and levers that brought our amazing vehicle to a stop. "Highgate Cemetery, as is."

Slipping free the brass goggles I wear whilst soldering, I obliged to replace the welding iron within its holder. Completion of my latest invention would require a postponement. Duty called.

"Punctual as always, Styx," I remarked favorably, my pocket watch asserting that it was midnight. The witching hour.

Adjusting my top hat, I slid free the exit hatch and leaped out.

With aid of my cane, I abseiled with perceived speed down the mooring cable. There were but mere seconds to admire the pristine night sky before plunging into throat-burning smog.

"Ten ages I have awaited for you to arrive," purred a voice tinted with devilish hate, consequent to my landing within the aforementioned cemetery.

There to greet me was a locust-legged form wrapped in a black cloak; upon his head a helmet of ghastly design. Through the eye slits burned satanic hellfire.

"A woman's prerogative is to be fashionably late," I replied with asperity, we two combatants warily circling each other.

"The police gazette offers grim intelligence that you have added two more unfortunates to the list, Jack," I continued. "So you and I must assuredly do final battle."

Suffice to say, honored society members, I shall, with some alacrity, pass over the following hours of bloody battle that did then elapse.

I had to bethink myself whether resolution would ever come and, my attention so engaged, failed to escape a blast of blue-and-white flame from Jack's mouth.

With me momentarily blinded, Jack thought he had, at last, triumphed! Through blurred vision, I saw him leap a full fifteen feet in the air to bring down upon me a deadly blow.

"My dear Jack," said I, peeling from my shoulder a mystical tattoo. "I entreat you, do not crow as yet."

With that, I tossed the symbol into Jack's path. A magical portal opened, and Jack fell through, screaming obscenities the like of which a lady had never heard!

SPRING-HEELED JACK FACT FILE

Location: The United Kingdom, United States, and India

Appearance: Tall, bugly (butt-ugly) dude in a cloak (and sometimes a helmet)

Strength: Well, his leg power is phenomenal!

Weaknesses: Mystical weapons—but you'll have to ask him to stand still first!

Powers: Superleap, superspeed, razor claws, supernatural flame from mouth and/or chest

Fear Factor: 31

PROFIT FROM SPRING-HEELED JACK

Hire him out as a window cleaner for high-rise office buildings!

WEEKLY WORLD
EXAMINER
THE WORLD'S MOST RELIABLE NEWSPAPER

ALL NEW!
STRANGE UNEXPECTED BIZARRE and all TRUE

WEREWOLF RUNS AMOK
EXCLUSIVE REPORT BY NEELA NIGHTSHADE

DEMON BABY
THWARTS NUCLEAR BOMB PLOT
PICTURES INSIDE

The Numero Uno Emperor of savage, howling, flesh-snacking therianthropes out there is both your favorite and ours—the werewolf!

But there's also a myriad motley collection of were-bears, were-jaguars, were-hyenas, were-bulls, were-crocodiles, were-hares, were-foxes, were-raccoons, were-badgers (we *aren't* making this up!), were-deer, were-moose, were-seals, were-rats, were-owls, and were-goodness-knows-what!

No matter which country you're in, there's a rank were-beastie awaiting to feast on you!

The preeminent (primary) form of therianthropy is *lycanthropy*, the human-into-ravaging-wolf-hybrid combo.

(FYI: The term *lycanthrope* comes from the ancient Greek word *lykánthropos*—literally, "wolf man.")

Then we have *cynanthropy*, which covers all the types of rabid human-to-dog weirdos, and *ailuranthropy* for the human-to-cat-lovers among you!

Hold your were-horses, you cry! Where did all these were-things originate, anyhow?

Human-to-animal shape-shifters have been around ever since cave dudes first started wearing animal fur as the latest must-have fashion accessory.

Bad move! Why? When the aboriginal (the earliest of its kind found in a region) people of Africa and the Americas wanted to thank their ancient gods for a bountiful harvest and various whatnot they would *parrr-tyyy on down* with hard-core spiritual ceremonies, wearing the skins of the animals they had killed.

During said ceremonies, the fur-wearers would take on aspects of the animal. Over the centuries, strands of animal DNA mixed with human DNA to eventually transform man into beast!

(Biology note: DNA, short for the decidedly less cool *deoxyribonucleic acid*, is the hereditary—passed from parents to children, 50 percent each from mom and pop—material found in all living organisms, including monsters and humans.)

You already know that we humans share between 95 to 98 percent of our DNA with chimps, but some current estimates also reckon that our DNA is approximately 99 percent compatible with mice, 90 percent with cats, 85 percent compatible with dogs and zebra fish, 80 percent with cows, 70 percent with sea sponges, 60 percent with fruit flies, and 40 percent with the humble mushroom!

The religious Crusades of the eleventh through thirteenth centuries saw Europeans trampling across other people's continents to hack 'n' slash Christianity to the masses.

In doing so, the hidden were-beasts followed them back home and they were soon popping up in Spain, Germany, France, and the United Kingdom! From there, it was a hop, skip, and a jump to the good ol' US of A!

Here's another shocking report from Neela Nightshade, ace reporter for the Weekly World Examiner!

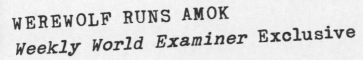

WEREWOLF RUNS AMOK
Weekly World Examiner Exclusive

Normandy, France, June 30

Each month on the three nights of the mystical "full moon," behind tightly bolted doors, terrified citizens of the quaint seventeenth-century town of Lyons-la-Forêt whisper desperate prayers for celestial protection.

Quivering uncontrollably, they await the ethereal cry of that royal denizen of the forest, the august wolf.

But this is no ordinary *Canis lupus*. This is *le loup-garou*——the werewolf!

Now, as the last wisps of twilight subtly merge with the encroaching darkness on the outskirts of town, I find myself on a nocturnal hunt through the dense Lyons forest, one of the largest ranges of beech trees in all of Europe.

The tree branches reach up high in religious supplication toward the majestic glowing orb suspended 238,900 miles above us.

Yet it is not the legendary *loup-garou* that this reporter is tracking; no, the animal I want to snare is far more bloodthirsty and dangerous. Its name is——MAN!

The forest floor is littered with steel log traps that have been set to catch the werewolf. Rich individuals who take twisted pleasure in wearing fur from a dead animal would pay much for its unique pelt.

More than fifty million animals worldwide are slaughtered every year simply for their fur. And this doesn't even account for the over *one billion* rabbits that are killed. Remind me again: *Who* is the real "animal"?!

My dark thoughts are pierced by a hideous howling close by! *Loup-garou?* No, the incessant, agonized screams are much too human!

Hurrying through the thicket, I burst into a clearing to find an overweight man whimpering on the ground, his leg crushed inside a steel-jawed animal trap!

"Sacré bleu! Helllp meeeeee!" he pitifully sobs.

I am about to give aid when I spot a rifle on the ground. The hunter has been caught in his own trap!

Another howling splits the warm night air. This one definitely isn't human!

A massive shape leaps from the bushes, its luxurious golden fur reflected in the moon's eerie light. This magnificent creature radiates immense power; its fangs drooling thick saliva, eyes glinting with ancient wisdom.

Surreptitiously, I press the camera button on my smartphone, bow respectfully, and withdraw back into the trees.

I make my way back to town, the terrified death screams that echo around the forest quickly dying away.

WERE-BEASTS FACT FILE

Location: The world (pop down any dark alley and you'll probably meet one!)

Appearance: All kinds of everything (but mostly hairy with sharp fangs and claws—oh, and halitosis! Oooh, man! Their breath stinks!)

Strength: Supernatural

Weaknesses: In human form—anything that can kill a human. As were-beasts—were-cats (silver), were-dogs (gold), were-birds (nickel and brass), were-reptiles (copper and mercury); decapitation, drowning, fire, falling from a great height

Powers: A werewolf bite turns you into one! Extended life (up to two thousand years or more); enhanced healing factor; animal-keen senses, including sight, smell, and hearing; superspeed (unless you're a were-slug!)

Fear factor: Werewolf/tiger/lion/shark/bear/gorilla, etc.—91.9; were-deer/raccoon/butterfly/worm/aphid, etc.—not so much! (By our reckoning? 0.3)

HOW TO KILL A WERE-SNAIL

CYCLOPS

Location: Greece
Appearance: Giant with one eye in the center of his forehead. First recorded by ancient Greek oral poet Hesiod, who was chilling sometime around 750 BC–650 BC. The three original cyclopes were called Brontes (thunder), Steropes (lightning), and Arges (bright).
Strength: Dude, they play "tag" with dragons!
Weaknesses: No depth perception (the ability to see in 3-D or judge the distance of objects), so incredibly clumsy. A poke in the eye with a sharp stick will do the trick.
Powers: Able to crush boulders with their bare hands!
Fear Factor: 31

CUEGLE

Location: The province of Cantabria in northern Spain
Appearance: Short dude with coal-black skin, a single horn in the center of its head, and three eyes colored green, red, and blue. Five sets of teeth. Long beard. Two legs, and three arms without hands.
Strength: Heavyweight
Weaknesses: Oak and holly leaves
Powers: Uses arms like clubs to smite its prey, or skewers them with its horn. Devours animals and human babies.
Fear Factor: For lil' munchkins—100!

DZIWOZONA

(aka Mamuna)

Location: Rivers, lakes, swamps, and streams in Slavic countries (such as Bulgaria, Croatia, the Czech Republic, Poland, and Russia)

Appearance: Either a baby-napping ugly old hag with green skin; a gross, hairy body; long hair; and breasts so large she uses them to wash her clothes. Or else a beautiful young woman. Whatever form, she will appear as either a little person or a giant, and sometimes wears a red hat with a fern twig stuck in it.

Strength: Human strength

Weaknesses: To save her kid from being snatched, a mother will tie a red ribbon around the baby's wrist, put a red hat on its head, and shield its face from the light of the moon. She must not wash its diapers after sunset or turn her head from the lil' munchkin when it is asleep. Only this will ward off the Dziwozona!

Powers: Shape-shifter. Once she's stolen a human baby, Dizzy will exchange it for one of her own offspring, which is hideously ugly and disfigured. We're talking Nightmare City!

Fear Factor: For moms—98.5

FACHAN

(aka Fachen, Fachin, or, um, Peg Leg Jack!)

Location: Caves of Scotland and Ireland

Appearance: Gruesomely ugly and fearsome dwarfish one-legged creep with one eye, a spiky tuft of hair or a mane of black feathers coming out of its head, a huge mouth, and most notably, a withered arm and hand bursting out of its chest! Boss!

Strength: Prodigious!

Weaknesses: A mud ball in the eye followed by a quick sword stroke to chop off its arm has always worked for us!

Powers: A deadly flail (chain) covered in iron apples, which it uses to destroy an entire orchard in one night. Its visage is so horrifying it can induce a fatal heart attack in humans. Will smite anyone who comes near its territory, and can swallow its victim whole. National hopping champ.

Fear Factor: 73.3

GROKE

Location: Finland
Appearance: Cutest bogeyman . . . sorry,
bogeywoman—ever!! Literally a giant blue blob
with eyes and mouth! You can't miss her!
Strength: Extremely soft and cuddly!
Weaknesses: More scared of humans than we
are of her! Utter, overwhelming, heartbreaking
loneliness—no one wants to be her friend! They all
run away! Everyone go: awww!!
Powers: Groke is so sad and alone that the very
ground beneath her feet freezes as she walks.
(Anyone got a tissue handy? *SNIFF!*)
Fear Factor: -5,000,000!!

HARIONAGO

(aka Harionna)
Location: The Ehime Prefecture region, island of
Shikoku, Japan
Appearance: Beautiful woman with freaky long,
serpentine, sentient hair, the ends of which are
tipped with piercing thornlike barbs
Strength: Nothing special
Weaknesses: A large pair of beauty scissors or a
ginormous bottle of hair remover
Powers: Loves to waylay young men and laugh
at them. If they laugh back, Harionago sets her
loony locks onto them, wrapping them up tight
before stabbing them to death—verrry slowly!
Fear Factor: 14.8

JACK-IN-IRONS

Location: The country back roads of Yorkshire, England

Appearance: Ghost-giant combo! Dressed in all black robes, jolly Jack's fashion accessories include thick iron chains wrapped around his body, attached to the heads of his victims. He also carries an extremely large wooden club with iron spikes.

Strength: Hey, dude, he's a GIANT!!

Weaknesses: If you discover his Achilles' heel—his major weakness—let us know!

Powers: The power to scare the sweet bejeebers outta English country folk!

Fear Factor: 57

ONOCENTAUR

Location: Aegean, Ionian, and Mediterranean Seas around Greece

Appearance: Man-donkey (Okay, stop snickering!! Very self-conscious about his looks is our Ono!) The hairy man top half is rational; the ashen-colored quadruped (four-footed) donkey bottom half extremely wild. (You would be, too, if you looked like he does!)

Strength: Violent temper. Superpowered back kick. Able to smash holes in the hulls of wooden ships!

Weaknesses: Cannot abide captivity and will purposely starve itself to death!

Powers: Works in conjunction with the sirens to attack Greek ships and drown all on board. Preferred weapons of choice are the bow and club. Speedy swimmer. Never sleeps. Ever.

Fear Factor: 34

RUURUHI KEREPOO

Location: New Zealand
Appearance: Hideous, ugly, deformed cannibalistic hag with large mouth and fangs. Gross, hairy hands and razor-sharp talons. Piercing, thick spines protruding all over her body. Directs her hatred toward the long-suffering Maori people. (Cultural note: The Maori people first landed on New Zealand from the 1,000-plus islands of Polynesia around AD 1300.)
Strength: Extreme!
Weaknesses: A spear (if you can get close enough)
Powers: Uses talons to decapitate young girls from the Maori tribe before eating their fresh, tender flesh. (Yum!) Superstrong spines ward off attacks. Although blind, her acute hearing and smell allow her to sense where her victims are hiding!
Fear Factor: For the Maori—77.7

SHIRIME

Location: Japan
Appearance: Um . . . er . . . how can we put this politely? Mischievous, featureless, and totally naked dude apparition who bends over to reveal a large, bright yellow eye pushing itself outta his butt! (Yes, yes! We know! Ewww!)
Strength: Oh, come on! Butt-Eye Man?! Don't think so!
Weaknesses: Finds his butt blocked when he's desperate for a number two!
Powers: Can look both ways at the same time!
Fear Factor: -144.1

SPHINX

Location: Greece (Betcha thought we were going to say Egypt, didn't ya? Ha! Some monster hunter you are! The one in Egypt is male!)

Appearance: Female! The head of a beautiful woman and body of a lion, along with eagle wings and the tail of a snake or dragon. (FYI: The Sphinx is the more intelligent cousin to the Manticore.) Her name comes from the Greek word *sphingo*, which means "to strangle."

Strength: Ravaging!

Weaknesses: Seriously poor loser! She hates it when a human beats her at her own game, which is . . .

Powers: Death riddles. She stops travelers and asks them a riddle. If they get it wrong—whammo! They are killed and then eaten! Also, in case you escape that little inescapable death trap, a bad-luck curse! (The "trip over a small twig and fall over a cliff to the jagged rocks below" type of bad luck, not the "Oh poo! My lottery numbers didn't come up this week!" type.)

Fear Factor: 86.1

YELLOW CAT VAMPIRE

(aka Sari-Kedi)

Location: The rural fields of Europe

Appearance: Stunning young woman with jet-black or gold hair that reaches down to her waist, and hypnotic emerald-green cat's eyes. When the wind shrieks and the owls screech on moonless nights, the Yellow Cat Vampire makes her appearance!

Strength: Gripping!

Weaknesses: Catnip, balls of wool, squeaky mouse toys—she can't resist them!

Powers: Shape-shifter. Hypnotic singing and mesmeric stare. Young men who hear the Yellow Cat Vampire's enchanted voice are unable to resist rushing into her welcoming arms . . . and are usually never seen alive again! (Those that do survive are left as shriveled husks, their hair turned white from heart-scaring terror!)

Fear Factor: 42

(Research note: Check out the epic ballad written in honor of the Yellow Cat Vampire by poet Frederick William von Herbert in his book *By-paths in the Balkans*, published in 1906!

ANIMAL HORRORS

Everything you can imagine is real.

—Pablo Picasso (born Pablo Ruiz y Picasso, 1881-1973)

—Spanish painter and sculptor

We've already covered what cryptids are in our companion book *Monster Hunters Unlimited: The Undead and Water Beasts.*

But for those who came in late to the party (what kept you?!), here's some down and dirty intel on these fantabulous legendary vicious varmints and mammalian monstrosities!

Cryptozoology and cryptobotany (from the Greek word *krypto,* meaning "hidden"— and no, it has nothing to do with a flying pooch!) are branches of science that investigate strange animals and plants of which there is no actual evidence of their existence. (We've said it before—just because there's no proof, doesn't mean it isn't there!)

Such a list would include everyone's favorite cryptids like Bigfoot, the Loch Ness Monster, those hideous hellhounds, and the Jersey Devil. (Three of which are covered in this section! How's that for service?)

Many creatures that were once derided as make-believe are now known to be real!

Early European explorers of Australia described one elusive "cryptid" they saw as having a head like a deer, yet standing upright like a man and hopping about like a frog. Any takers? Yup, a kangaroo! Some cryptid! Sheesh!

Other once-cryptids include the bizarre-looking platypus (said to be a cross between a duck and a mole!), the okapi, the Komodo dragon, the giant squid and giant panda—and even the mountain gorilla! We have a totally out-there theory about the more violent and vicious monster cryptids that prowl the earth. Want to hear it? Sure you do!

Some people reckon it's Mother Nature's neat if kind of twisted revenge on humanity for our ongoing cruelty and exploitation of wildlife and nature!

Fancy having shampoo or battery acid squirted in your eyes? No? Well, nor do animals in unnecessary experiments!

And apparently they're not really chill about being stuck behind bars or forced to perform unnatural tricks for someone's warped entertainment.

Of course, like humans, some cryptids are mean and nasty for the sake of it, and it's these animal horrors that we, as dedicated monster hunters, have sworn to track down, capture, and, if necessary—kill. (Hey, humans are animals, too! Sometimes even *they* need protecting!)

Stone-cold killers like the cockamamie European Cockatrice, the bird with the petrifying stare that turns flesh into stone! (Check out our astonishing case study about a Cockatrice's recent attack on Buckingham Palace! It's a shocker!)

And Kongamato, the bioluminescent African flying reptile that likes to overturn boats and chow down on the passengers!

Then there's the terrifying Japanese ghost chicken Basan, the giant French snail Lou Carcolh—the mollusk as big as a hill!—and the totally terrifying Bonnacon: half-bull, half-goat, with an attack method so disgusting we really shouldn't mention it! (But hey, you know us!)

And who can forget the unforgettable Mongolian death worm and the ever-deranged Asian Vegetable Lamb?! (Okay, that last one is sort of silly, but hey—with a name like that, we had to include him!)

So grab your passport and make ready for a worldwide trip to track down some of the most horrific animal horrors that ever lived! (And some undead ones, too!)

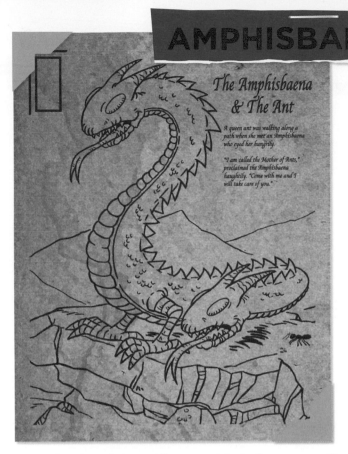

The Amphisbaena & The Ant

A queen ant was walking along a path when she met an Amphisbaena who eyed her hungrily.

"I am called the Mother of Ants," proclaimed the Amphisbaena haughtily. "Come with me and I will take care of you."

First up on our wanders through the world's most malefic (evil) menagerie of freaky-deak animal horrors that crawl, slither, swim, jump, wiggle, slide, and charge across This Savage Earth, we have the not-so-wee-heasties who never know whether they're coming or going!

The amphisbaenae (plural; Latin for "walking both ways") originate in the deserts of North Africa.

The creature has two heads, one at either end of an elongated serpent body. Or . . . a double-ended horned dragon's head and scaled body with chicken's feet and oversize bat and/or feathered wings. And its eyes glow like candles!

It's kind of hard to get exact intel on this monster because if you're unlucky enough to come across an amphisbaena, you're already dead! Sucky!

71

Whatever. Before you try to capture or kill one, check out its mental party trick. When threatened, the ampy will bite down its double jaws on tail and neck, creating a wheel-shaped body which it uses to roll at blurring speeds across the desert floor! Righteous!

It can also move backward or forward, excrete a deadly poison from skin and fangs, hypnotize its prey, and even kill on eye contact—but only during a full moon. Word to the wise: There are sometimes *two* full moons in one month!

(Astronomy note: The second of two full moons that appear during the same month, or the fourth full moon that appears in one season, is known as a *blue moon*. This epic event happens, on average, every two or three years, and a *double* blue moon—two in one year—is even rarer, occurring once every nineteen years, and usually in January and March, due to the short month of February. The next double blue moon? The year 2018! Sad to say, a *blue moon* is just an expression. The moon doesn't really turn blue! Bummer!)

Born from the dripping blood from the head of the totally freaky snake-haired monster Medusa (which the ancient Greek mythological hero Perseus lopped off during battle), the amphisbaenae's favorite Dish of the Day is the rotting bodies of soldiers killed in battle.

They are also partial to a plate of ants and are oftentimes referred to as the Mother of Ants. (Yes, we *know* that at least half of the amphisbaenae are male—hey, we didn't come up with the silly moniker!)

Case Study 116/38A

Aesop's Fables is a series of short tales, usually featuring anthropomorphic animals (animals that act like humans, wicked-cool cartoon characters being a prime example) with a kick-in-the-butt moral message.

Legend has it that they were first created by an Ethiopian slave named Aesop who lived in ancient Greece between 620 BC and 560 BC. (History note: The Greek word for Ethiopia was Aethiops.)

Over six hundred fables are credited to Aesop, yet since he never wrote any down it was up to later scholars to record these stories for prosperity. This guarantees that not all the fables were actually created by Aesop.

We've unearthed one of Aesop's lesser-known fables. Was it written by the awesome-sauce dude himself? That's up to you to decide!

THE AMPHISBAENA & THE ANT

A queen ant was walking along a path when she met an amphisbaena who eyed her hungrily.

"I am called the Mother of Ants," the amphisbaena haughtily proclaimed. "Come with me and I will feed you well."

"I am not that foolish," said the queen ant. "I know you want to eat me. But I am the mother of all the hundreds of ants in my colony. Come home with me and you can eat them all, so long as you allow me to live."

The amphisbaena agreed, and the pair traveled together to a nearby tree. A large nest hung from a branch.

"My colony lives in that nest," said the queen ant. "If I were you, I would place one of my mouths at the top of the nest and the other mouth at the bottom of the nest to stop them from escaping."

The amphisbaena did as instructed. He raised both heads to the nest and covered either end with his mouths. He sucked hard, intending to swallow all of the ants in one go.

Moments later, he was writhing on the ground, screaming in pain.

"Ahhh! I have sharp stabbing pains in my stomach!" he wailed. "It hurts most dreadfully!"

The pain was so great, the amphisbaena died. The queen ant watched as dozens of angry wasps crawled out of his open mouth.

"Dear me," said the queen ant, looking across to the anthill that stood on the ground near the tree. "I seem to have made a terrible mistake."

Moral: Don't believe everything you are told.

(Now try writing your own Aesop's fable!)

AMPHISBAENA FACT FILE

Location: Deserts of North Africa, most notably Libya

Appearance: Two-headed serpent, dragon, or combo of the two; with or without horns; bird's feet; and bat or bird wings

Strength: The small ones are puny, the big ones not so much

Weaknesses: They can be captured or killed quite easily with most traps and weapons

Powers: The power to look both ways simultaneously! Superspeed rolling! Deadly poison and gaze! (Note: Wearing the skin of an amphisbaena can cure many ailments, including arthritis, rheumatism, and even the common cold!)

Fear Factor: If you're dead—100; but then, hey, you're dead . . . !

HOW TO KILL AN AMPHISBAENA

Carve thousands of ant models from rock and leave them out for the amphisbaena to eat. It will then be too heavy to move, and you can safely approach and chop off its heads!

Next up is the rinky-dink, popping-fresh, and downright freak-the-mind legendary bovine that has the most awesome-sauce defense/attack abilities of *all* monsters—of any type!

And we guarantee you'll *never* guess what they are!

Energy beams from the eyes? Hmm, kind of silly and . . . *nah!*

A mystical sonic scream that opens a portal to the Dark Dimension? Nope!

The ability to adhere to solid surfaces, allowing it to climb walls and hang from ceilings? Oh, come on! Now that's just being silly!

When startled, the shy and retiring Bonnacon (aka Bonacon, Bonasus or Vilde Kow) will lift up a back leg and let out a hot, blistering, poisonous fart that KILLS!!! IN!!! SECONDS!!!

But that's like nothing compared to the Bonnacon's greatest weapon!

If threatened by hunters, it will strain really hard before spraying out searing napalm-strength caustic poo over a length of 1,760 feet and covering two acres, which is just a little shorter than two football fields!

And whatever it touches—human, animal, or plant—will immediately burst into flame! *Whoooossh!*

For those of you not *au fait* (French for *at fact*, i.e., knowledgeable) about napalm, it is one of the sickest, most twisted and wicked (and we don't mean this in a good way!) of humanity's diabolical killing weapons ever created.

Inspired by the "sticky fire" incendiary weapons created by the ancient Greeks (ca. AD 672), American chemist Louis Fieser (1899–1977) invented napalm in 1942.

A gelling agent of naphthenic acid and palmitic acid mixed with petroleum, this foul stuff sticks to the skin and will burn down to the bone! (Napalm creates temperatures of between 1,500–2,200°F. By comparison, water boils at 212°F!)

It was first used against Japanese cities during World War II.

Other countries went on to use napalm in many subsequent wars, most notably the Korean War (1950–1953) and the Vietnam War (1954–1975), and this diabolical weapon is still being used in wars today.

Mr. know-it-all ancient Roman author, naturalist, philosopher, and navy and army commander Pliny the Elder (AD 23–AD 79; he died during the eruption of Mount Vesuvius on August 25) first mentioned the Bonnacon in his mega-epic encyclopedia, *Naturalis historia*, published between AD 77 and AD 79.

This book claims to cover all ancient knowledge and is still the model on which encyclopedias published today are based!

Pliny wrote: "There are reports of a wild animal in Paionia [author's note: a now-defunct independent kingdom in northern Greece] called the bonasus, which has the mane of a horse, but in all other respects resembles a bull; its horns are curved back in such a manner as to be of no use for fighting . . ."

More than a dozen other manuscripts over the centuries mention Ol' Bonnie, and he has a starring role in *The Aberdeen Bestiary*, a book published in England in AD 1200.

(A *bestiary*—or *Bestiarum vocabulum* for all you Latin freaks out there—is an illuminated manuscript that compiles the latest information on the fauna and flora of the day, usually accompanied by a religious moral lesson.)

We quote: "[The creature] . . . discharges fumes from the excrement of its belly over a distance of three acres, the heat of which sets fire to anything it touches."

So if you go hunting the Bonnacon, make sure you're not downwind of it!

Case Study 004/744B

Ranger Rich is the leader of the Junior Woodland Rangers chapter of the Woodland Guild.

He has kindly allowed us to reprint a chapter from his latest guide, *Ranger Rich's Wildfire Prevention Tips*, given out free to all members of the JWR.

Well, chums, so far I've taught you not to play with matches in the woods and how to safely build and put out a campfire without burning down your tent!

Now for an important message if you're traveling abroad, especially to one of the forty-eight countries that make up the amazing continent of Asia.

Asia is the world's largest continent and includes such countries as China, India, Indonesia, Japan, Pakistan, Iran, Iraq, Korea, part of Russia, and dozens more!

Asia has some of the largest forests and rainforests, although much of this pristine woodland has now sadly been destroyed by deforestation.

But there is a forest animal that even your pal Ranger Rick suggests his bestest buddies in the JWR stay well clear of—the Bonnacon!

This ferocious beast looks like an oversize goat or bull, and when it gets scared it does something terribly rude——it, um, "defecates" over great distances, and whatever this, er, "waste matter" touches, bursts into flame!

Not even a high-strength fire extinguisher can put out this supernatural fire, so don't even try. Phone the proper authorities to warn them and then run away!

But make sure you don't give out your real name, otherwise the authorities may think that YOU started the fire!

And then you'll be spending the next thirty years in a squalid Asian prison for arson!

BONNACON FACT FILE

Location: Countries of Asia
Appearance: Oversize bull/goat
Strength: Terrifying!
Weaknesses: An extremely sore backside that stops it from sleeping!
Powers: Long-distance fiery farts!
Fear Factor: 66.6

HOW TO DESTROY A BONNACON

Sneak up behind a sleeping Bonnacon and carefully slip a large cork up its butt. When it wakes and tries to fart, the napalm will be blocked inside and the Bonnacon will explode! Messy and extremely smelly, but hey——highly effective!

DANGER: FLATULENCE

When is a Basilisk not a Basilisk?

When it's a Cockatrice!

Don't worry if you get these two fowl, er, we mean *foul* fiends confused! Heck, even experienced monster hunters occasionally throw a foul ball with this one!

Secret tip: A Basilisk is created when a seven- or nine-year-old toad or serpent lays an egg on a dung hill and it is sat on by a rooster until it hatches. However, a Cockatrice is created when a similarly-aged rooster (keep reading!) lays an egg and it is sat upon by a toad. Simple!

"Um," we hear you say in puzzled voice. "How can a rooster—a *male*—lay eggs?" Hey, we are talking *monsters* here! Just go with the flow!

The Basilisk (from the Ancient Greek—yep, them dudes again!—*basilskos*, meaning "little king"), is believed to be the incarnation of the scary Death God!

It has a reptile's body and the face of either a rooster or truly ugly human.

Differences between this creepoid and the equally murderous Cockatrice? The Cockatrice has wings and clawed feet, while the Basilisk lacks either and has a crown or miter-shaped crest on its head.

(Religious note: A miter is the dopey ceremonial headgear worn by bishops, abbots, and whomever of various religious dominations.).

Both creatures are surprisingly small, not much larger than a real rooster. So why are these lil' pipsqueaks so pants-filling terrifying?

'Cause they possess a "to the max" dank and deadly . . . Death Stare! Yep, one look from these beasties and you'll be as dead as the Dodo!

Cockie can also kill by simply touching or breathing on ya—stinky breath or what?! And better yet, it possesses the spiffylicious power of *petrifaction*! (Petrifaction—aka petrification—is the power to turn living creatures to stone!)

Our old pal Pliny "I'm A Total Know-It-All!" the Elder, Ancient Roman nerd mentions both Basilisk and Cockatrice in his writings.

Of the Cockatrice, he writes: "Its touch and breath can scorch grass, kill bushes and burst rocks. Its poison is so deadly that once a man on a horse speared a cockatrice, the venom travelled up the spear and killed not only the man, but also the horse."

Luckily, there are a few good ways of dispatching these suckers!

First off, keep a weasel down your trousers 'cause those vicious furballs are immune to the Cockatrice's powers and can savage 'em to death!

And the cry of a real rooster will make a Cockatrice either run away in terror or it will kill it, um, "stone" dead!

Case Study 739/80

Here is the original broadcast transcript from Channel 10 News concerning an attack by a Cockatrice on the home of a VIP (Very Important Person) in London!

Here are some of the technical terms used in the script:

ON CAM: The newscaster speaking in the studio to camera

TAKE TAPE: Start of news-video footage

AERIAL SHOT: Shot taken from high above, by a helicopter

VO: Voice of the newscaster over the video footage

INT./EXT: Interior/Exterior shot

C/U: Close-up shot

[Editor's instructions in brackets]

TAPE OUT: End of the video footage

On Cam

This is Channel 10 News at eleven. I'm Robin Prentiss in for Kaci Bell. Our top news story: Terror at Buckingham Palace.

O.O. Take tape [Editor: at :00 show Aerial shot of BP video]

VO

London, England. Early this morning at Buckingham Palace, home to Her Majesty Queen Elizabeth II . . . ,

[Editor: at 09 int. BP statue of corgi]

two sentries, three servants, and one of her monarch's prized corgi dogs were found in various stages of petrifaction.

[Editor: at 15 show int. BP——darkened room]

Channel 10 spoke exclusively to one of the queen's children, who asked not to be identified.

[Editor: at 20 show C/U of PC——blur image]

"By jove, this is all rather frightful, what! Mummsie is most distressed at losing her corgi. Nowadays one is not safe even in one's own home."

[Editor: at 27 show artist sketch of bird]

It appears that some type of large bird flew in through an open window and when cornered, began attacking the victims. Our reporter spoke to parlor maid Elsie Bowbells about the incident.

[Editor: at 36 show int. BP——maid]

"Gobsmacked, I wuz, guv! It looked, well, y'know, a bit like one of them daft farm birds, but then it, well, y'know, began shootin' strange rays from its, no joke, mate, eyes. Everyone who wuz struck turned to, gor blimey, stone. Luvaduck, it were, well, y'know, 'orrible! Gave me the right collywobbles, know wha' I'm sayin'?!"

[:50 tape out]
On cam

Apparently, when the police arrived on the scene, the bird had already flown away. More on this developing story later in the program.

COCKATRICE FACT FILE

Location: Most European countries
Appearance: Rooster/reptile mix
Strength: Puny
Weaknesses: Weasel, cry of real rooster. Also, carry a hand mirror with ya and hold it up to the Cockatrice. Its own gaze will reflect back at it and ZAAAM! Cockie gets a taste of its own medicine!
Powers: Death/turn-to-stone stare, deadly halitosis, oozes poison from its body (sounds like our old Phys. Ed. teacher! Man, was he rank! Ugh!)
Fear Factor: 49

WHAT TO DO WITH A CAPTURED COCKATRICE

Hire it out to gangsters. Instead of wasting their ill-gotten gains by making concrete boots for their enemies, the Cockatrice will do it for them!

GREAT NAKED BEAR

Those of an easily embarrassed disposition may wish to pass on hunting our next monster!

Like his name suggests, this bestial bruin behemoth appears to its victims completely, utterly *nekid*! We know! Disgusting! No sense of shame, some monsters!

The Great Naked Bear (from now on referred to as GNB, because if you think we're going to keep writing out his full moniker, you don't know us too well!) terrorizes, savages, and devours members of the Seneca, Cayuga, and Iroquois tribes across the vast forests of North America.

The GNB has many tags, depending upon which tribe you hail from.

Usually his name is pronounced *Nyah-gwah-heh* or *Gah-nyah-gweah-heh-goh-wah*, or simply Fred to his friends.

The name comes from his ghastly appearance. Not only is the GNB a towering mammoth with a gigantic head, but he has no fur—at all! He's as bald as a billiard ball!

(Hairstyling note: Baldness—aka *alopecia*—affects both men and women. One in four men will start losing their hair before they are even twenty-one, and two-thirds of men will have some noticeable baldness by the time they are thirty-five!)

There are a number of factors that cause alopecia in humans, including your genes, diet, lifestyle, and the environment. But the poor GNB's baldness embarrassment is caused by eating—human flesh!

He can't resist it! If he simply ate more fruit and veggies and stopped snacking down on humes, he'd be as hairy as the next bear!

(Nature note: There are eight species of bear, all of which are omnivores; they eat both animal protein and vegetation. *Omnivore* literally means "all eater." Bears are shy creatures and understandably scared of humans. Less than a handful of humans are killed by bears each year—shame we can't say the same for the opposite statistic! Leave bears alone and they'll leave you alone. Simple, really.)

While a black bear can run at thirty miles per hour, a GNB is almost twice as fast, reaching speeds of fifty miles per hour, and can smell his next victim from a great distance. If confronted by a GNB, **DO NOT!!** climb a tree to escape. He will simply shake the tree until you fall out again!

Almost invincible, there is only one thing that will kill a GNB—but you'll have to wait for the Fact File to find out!

Case Study 118/3GNB

The pilgrims were an English religious sect who couldn't accept the teachings of the Church of England in the early 1600s and decided to head for pastures new.

They set sail from the port of Southampton, England, in the now legendary ship *The Mayflower*, on September 16, 1620.

After a grueling sixty-five days at sea (you try living squashed together with one hundred other people with no bathroom facilities! Yowsers!), they finally sighted land.

After a month of exploring the coastline, they chose Plymouth Rock as a suitable place for their settlement, and on December 16 dropped anchor. (And once on land created the first-ever and longest line for the bathroom!)

Long story short, after a hard winter the dudes survived and were soon colonizing other parts of the country. (Whether the Native Americans wanted them to or not!)

Here is an extract (complete with original spellings—and you thought your literary skills were bad!) believed to be from the diary of a pilgrim from a colony that mysteriously disappeared, never again to be seen!

All that was found of their existence was a severed, bloodied hand clutching a Bible! Spooky!

Des. 15 1622

The Horror of the Devill came upon us one wekke pastt.

Shuch was the grislie find made in the woodes close to camp. Mr. Cantorum, the firste of our peopl to fall, his blodded and ravished bodie torne unto shrodes.

Thence came sightings of a forme of great malignancie of beinge.

A giant beare with enlarged heade, and bodie naked of any covering. If shuch a creature existes, it is a Beast of the Antichrist indeede!

I am nowe the last of our comunitie and withe no foode left to fill my hungrie bellie I sit hear outside of camp reading from the Good Booke and readie to meett my fate which restes on Gods divine providente.

I have since hearde a great and strange crie which I knowe to be the same voce I had heard in the nightt, worst still than the crie of the dreadfull Iroquois Indeans, whom we have, of latte, cleared frome this area, it pleasing God to vanquish our enemie.

It rests now that I speake my final words. I hea heavie footfalls approaching from behind me, and growlings that threatene to overwhelm my senses withe terrors unimagined. I will not flinch, even unto dea

It is here the diary entry ended. The fate of the pilgrim who wrote it remains a mystery!

GREAT NAKED BEAR FACT FILE

Location: Forests of North America
Appearance: Big-headed naked bear—what more do you want?!
Strength: Monster-bear powerful!
Weaknesses: Arrows through the sole of his foot—the "weakness" to this weakness being that you have to convince the dude to lie down first!
Powers: Practically invincible (except for the arrows part)
Fear Factor: For prudes who don't appreciate the beauty of the naked form—100. And even for the rest of us—88.8!

HOW TO CAPTURE GNB

Have the police arrest the Great Naked Bear for public indecency! He'll go down for at least five years!

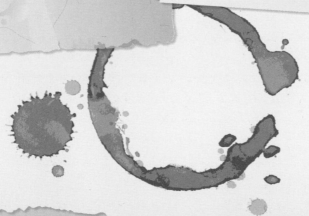

DIGEST of the UNCANNY & SUPERNATURAL

The Arcane Times

Two Pence

**JULY Lady Theodora Bennett 1838
Thwarts Devil Dog Attack
On The Coronation**

THINGS KEPT SECRET FROM THE W

Sighted on almost every continent, the location of preference for these ginormous and somewhat petrifying pooches of the supernatural world is the desolate moors and foghound country lanes of the sumptuously spooktacular British Isles!

These ethereal apparitions are crepuscular by habit (animals mostly active during the twilight hours of dusk and dawn, including the likes of rabbits, rats, wallabies, hamsters, guinea pigs, cats, moose, deer, bears, and various birds and insects) and always appear canine in form.

With fiery red or yellow eyes and a thick coat of stygian black fur, their alternate appellation (name) is, unsurprisingly—black dogs!

Possessed of superspeed and superstrength, these mutant mutts let off such a foul odor of burning brimstone that plants and grass within the surrounding area wither and die!

They are considered "the bearers of death" for the obvious reason—if you see one, your time is up!

The daddy of all spectral hellhounds is the multi-headed Cerberus, who often guards the entrance to Hades, and is sometimes seen with as many as fifty heads! This dude is skyscraper-tall and appears with either mane or tail made of writhing snakes!

Great news for monster hunters! Cerberus aside, there is a vast cornucopia (abundance) of these deadly doggies to track down!

In the United Kingdom alone they have Black Shuck, who is regularly sighted in East Anglia; the headless Whist Hounds of Cornwall; and the invisible, chain-rattling Barghest of Yorkshire!

Scottish people quake in fear with the coming of the green-furred, bull-size Cu Sith, and in Wales, the "mirror-eyed" Cŵn Annwn!

Elsewhere, there's the Rongeur d'Os (aka "gnawer of bones") of Normandy in northern France; the shape-changing Kludde of Belgium; and in the Catalan areas of Spain and France, the blood-sucking vampiric Dip!

The Japanese are fated to die by the paws of the Inugami, while the nerve-shattered inhabitants of the US states of Georgia and South Carolina bar their doors at night in fear of the appearance of Plat-Eye!

And how could anyone forget the totally awesome devil voodoo dogs of New Orleans, which are actually—zombies!

Case Study 666/6H

The most famous and exciting Black Dog fictional story was *The Hound of the Baskervilles*, written by Scottish physician and writer Sir Arthur Ignatius Conan Doyle (1859-1930) and featuring his famous Victorian detective, Sherlock Holmes.

The story was first serialized in the popular British fiction publication *Strand Magazine*, between August 1901 and April 1902, and is rightly regarded as a classic of the supernatural crime genre.

Here is an excerpt from an article written by Victorian adventuress Lady Theodora Bennett, for the investigative paranormal magazine *The Arcane Times*, on her own meeting with a hellhound!

[Thursday 28 June, 1838]

Adjusting my brass demon-hunting night-vision goggles, I locked eyes with the three-headed monstrosity and quipped, "So, Cerberus, you thrice-cursed stream of searing effluence from the rotting bowels of Satan's posterior, we are acquainted again."

"The pleasure is yours, Lady Theodora," barked the fetid cur in soulless symphony. "My pleasure will be in your death!"

Hellhounds have a proclivity to frequent sacred places such as graveyards, or at crossroads whereat Fate tosses life's Duplicitous Dice of Destiny.

One such divergence of paths as we now did intersect, wherein seven and one half hours hence would pass the gold-encrusted coach of the new queen as it took her to her ceremonial coronation at Westminster Abbey.

If Victoria were to unfortunately perish this day, my automated clockwork astrological globe predicted that blight and disaster would follow. The sun would, at last, go down on the great British Empire.

Cerberus was there to assure that such a circumstance took place; I to assure that it did not.

My pocket watch chimed three. The moon's waxing first quarter reflected light from the brass railings that stood in mute attention along the Mall to encourage crowd control once the colorful procession began.

"You cannot stop my master, Theodora," barked Cerberus, its triple vocal chords reverberating painfully through my head. "He always wins."

Wrinkling my nose at the charnel stench emanating from Cerberus's bottom, I pulled free the psionic purifier blunderbuss from inside my overbust corset and blasted the devil dog with a mystical charge that could have split an atom asunder. *CHOOOOM!*

It did not, I am of melancholy manner to reveal, succeed in its mission.

"Foolish mortal!" raged Cerberus. "I am undead and cannot therefore die! Unlike, I deem to suggest——you!"

Upon whence came threefold blasts of blistering hellfire hurled from his mouths, singeing my hair as I backflipped from yon frenzied attack!

"Good doggy! Open wide!" laughed I, tossing three small, calcified meat bones into the open orifices.

Gulping down the proffered morsels, Cerberus was about to resume attack when I checked again my pocket watch.

"Three . . . two . . . one!" I counted down and dived for cover.

The Imploders, as I am proudly wont to call my little inventions, triggered an implosion inside Cerberus's stomach that sucked the demon beast into dimensions unknown.

Where Cerberus had stood was now nothing but a large, smoking hole in the road.

With nationalistic fervor I raised my top hat and cried, "God save the Queen!"

HELLHOUNDS FACT FILE

Location: Everywhere!
Appearance: Hellish black dog between the size of a horse and a small mountain, of satanic appearance
Strength: Unearthly!
Weaknesses: If they try to cross running water they go POOOF and disappear!
Powers: Death stare, shape-changing, shadow travel, super-speed and superstrength, occasional flight abilities soul-gathering, brimstone farts.
Fear Factor: 100!

HOW TO GET RID OF A HELLHOUND

Lure it to a water park and trick it into going down the log flume!

JERSEY DEVIL

One question repeatedly asked of monster hunters is, "Where the heck do all these monsters and cryptids come from, anyhow?"

Some beasties are created through magic spells and curses, others originate from alternate dimensions. There are man-made terrors and those that were created in the blistering bowels of hell itself.

And then we have the North American Jersey Devil. The monster born—of woman!

The seriously spooky Pine Barrens encompasses seven counties and 22 percent of New Jersey's entire land area. That's a whopping two thousand square miles, or 1.1 million acres, of great oak, cedar, and—surprise!—pine trees, the most predominant of which is *Pinus rigida*, better known as pitch pine.

As legend has it, sometime in the early 1700s, an English woman named Deborah Smith came to North America and married some poor slob name Leeds.

Poverty-stricken, they lived in a ramshackle dwelling in the swamp-infested Pine Barrens where the now Mrs. Leeds gave birth, in quick succession, to twelve kids!

When, in 1735, she discovered that she was pregnant for the thirteenth time, Mother Leeds supposedly cried out, "I don't want any more children! Let it be a devil!" Oops!

It isn't wise to take the devil's name in vain, and when the kid was born, one dark and stormy night, it was hideously deformed. He later grew wings and flew up the chimney, never to return!

Other legends have it that Mrs. L. was an actual witch and the baby's pa was the devil himself!

Or that she was an American woman who married a British soldier during the Revolutionary War of 1775–1783 (when America won its independence from Great Britain), and her traitorous liaisons with the enemy created the Jersey Devil!

The kid was either born with a serpentine or goat's body, a horse's head and hooves, bat wings, and a forked tail.

Or he had the head of a collie dog with wings and cloven feet!

Or a kangaroo's or elephant's body!

Oh, and he had glowing eyes and a piercing scream!

Whatever. Once born, the creature took off and hid out in the Barrens, feasting on small children and livestock.

There have been more than two thousand sightings of the Jersey Devil in the succeeding centuries!

In 1820, Joseph Bonaparte (1766–1844), former king of Spain and elder bro of emperor Napoléon Bonaparte (1769–1821; the infamous French military

A FACE ONLY A MOTHER COULD LOVE!

and political leader and oftentimes megalomaniac who tried to enslave continental Europe during the Napoleonic Wars of 1803–1815), sighted the Jersey Devil numerous times while out hunting in the Barrens.

In 1909, over one thousand people from New Jersey to Philadelphia saw the creature during the one-week period of January 16–23!

And as recently as February 2011, the Jersey Devil was spotted in Miami enjoying a well-deserved vacation from the harsh New Jersey winters!

Case Study 977/4JD

Tobias Toombes is a thirteen-year-old monster hunter who posts a weekly blog.

A MONSTER HUNTER'S BLOG

Yo, homies! Being a world-class monster hunter isn't all fame, glamor 'n' hanging out with the latest celebs!

Case in point: Last night found this monster hunter wading waist-deep in the stinky, bloodred swamp waters of New Jersey's Pine Barrens, using a very long stick to poke aside icky unmentionables you wouldn't find in the dankest of city sewers! Gross!

A little while back, some dopey lil' kid had wandered off and his gas-bloated corpse was found floating facedown in these very swamps, his throat ripped out and deep chew marks tattooing his remains.

The locals reckon the terrifying Jersey Devil is again on the prowl!

So naturally, I decided to eyeball the scene for myself. (The oldies think I'm off on a weekend camping trip with the Scouts—hey, works for me!)

Three hours of stumbling over stupid tree roots and losing my direction in the freezing phosphorescent green mist that had descended over the area, and I was about to call time on the expedition.

Then a piercing, ethereal howl echoed from the pines. A coyote, or . . . ?! With icy fear-sweat slip-sliding down my trembling spine, I scanned the area with my high-powered flashlight.

Reflected in its brilliance was a huge mix 'n' match shape: part horse, part goat, with curved horns and oversize wings!

I had found—the Jersey Devil!

Staggering back, I tripped over a rock, landing hard on my butt, my hand wrapping itself around a thick tree branch!

Before the ugly monstrosity could make me its next meal, I javelin-ed the branch and watched in satisfaction as it pierced the creature's chest! THUNK!

Stupid not being my middle name—and in case it were only wounded—I skedaddled at Mach 10 speed back the way I had come!

That weekend, I was on monster-hunter sites, crowing about my titanic battle with JD, when some dude uploaded a photo.

It was of a large billboard standing on the outskirts of the Barrens that was promoting the existence of the Jersey Devil for the tourists.

The image of the creature had a large tree branch sticking through its chest!

Aww, shoot!

JERSEY DEVIL FACT FILE

Location: The Pine Barrens in New Jersey
Appearance: Horse's or collie's head, with or without horns; glowing eyes; kangaroo/serpent/goat/elephant leathery body; cloven or horse's hooves; forked tail
Strength: Cannonballs and bullets bounce off its hide!
Weaknesses: None we know of—any takers?
Powers: Flight, superstrength, possible immortality
Fear Factor: 10 (Aww, c'mon! The critter's kind of cute!)

USE OF A JERSEY DEVIL

Use a captured Cockatrice to turn it to stone and use it as a doorstop. It makes a great conversation piece!

Another pop quiz, dudes and dudettes!

What animals existed *before* the dinosaurs and are still around today?

(FYI: Dinosaurs were the BMOC during the Mesozoic Era, which lasted from approximately 248 to 65 million years ago. This era is subdivided into three periods: the Triassic, Jurassic, and Cretaceous.)

Ten points if you shouted out, "Tuatara!" (Heck, for that one, we'll award you *fifty* points!)

And for those who ask, "What the heck is a tuatara?!" it's a really cool type of lizard found only in New Zealand, one that possesses a "third eye" in its forehead!

The 445-million-year-old horseshoe crab wins you another ten points, and the fishy coelacanth, dating back 440 million years, ratchets you up another twenty!

The fifty species of eel-like, jawless lamprey, dating back at least 360 million years ago and *still* sucking on the blood of other marine fish like some gross vampiric sea monsters, wins you the game! Respect!

But we're betting not one of you called out: kongamato!

Once sharing the oppressive Mesozoic skies with its fellow pterosaur brethren, kongamato somehow survived the natural cataclysm—i.e., the dirty great asteroid that smashed into the Earth!—that wiped out 75 percent of all known species!

(Avian note: Pterosaurs were the first vertebrates—creatures with a backbone—that developed the ability to fly. The name originates from the ancient Greek word *pterosauros*, meaning "winged lizard.")

Today kongamato still totally owns the nocturnal airways of the Jiundu swamps of western Zambia, Angola, and the Democratic Republic of the Congo; Zimbabwe, Papua New Guinea, and areas of Cameroon, Tanzania, and Kenya, situated close to Mount Kilimanjaro and Mount Kenya.

There have also been sightings as far afield as South America, the United States, and Mexico! (Dude gets around!)

Kongamato is described by terrified villagers as a glow-in-the-dark (i.e., *bioluminescent*) reptile with a red or black body between four and seven feet in length; with a long, tapering head and tail; a mouth full of razor-sharp pointed teeth; and a wide, leathery wingspan of up to eight feet wide!

The name originates from its annoying habit of diving under the water and then speeding back up to the surface to capsize boats and drown the passengers, thus "breaker or overwhelmer of boats."

A cryptid with serious bad attitude, kongamato is mondo aggressive toward humans and can zap you with its "death stare," although rather than feast on live flesh it prefers to wait until a villager has kicked the bucket and been buried in the ground.

It then visits the cemetery at night to dig up and snack down on the rotting corpse! Juicy!

Case Study 336/22K

A flight data recorder (FDR) and cockpit voice recorder (CVR) are fitted to all commercial aircraft. They record flight details and communication between the flight crew and air traffic control.

When a serious incident occurs—such as a plane crash—the FDR and CVR are recovered and allow investigators to piece together what happened on that fateful journey.

(FYI: The devices are popularly known as the "black box." Although originally black, they are now bright orange or red. The black box prototype was invented by Australian scientist Dr. David Warren [1925–2010] in 1956.)

Here is a transcript allegedly from the CVR of Zambia Airways Flight ZA545, which crashed in the Jiundu swamps in 1984. All sixty-eight passengers and crew perished.

OCTOBER 3, 1984

JIUNDU SWAMPS, ZAMBIA
ZAMBIA AIRWAYS FLIGHT ZA545
ATRWING 977

17:41:17 CA This is ZULU ALPHA 545 to control. Can you confirm no known aircraft below three thousand?
17:41:39 ATC Affirmative. No known aircraft. What's the problem, guys?
17:42:23 CA There appears to be a small aircraft below three thousand moving at speed.
17:42:51 ATC What type of aircraft?
17:43:11 CA Cannot confirm. It appears to be . . .

17:43:27 COP What the ### is it? Is it . . . glowing?

17:43:38 ATC Glowing? You mean its landing lights are on? Confirm.

17:44:03 CA Heck, no! I mean, the aircraft itself is glowing . . . green . . .

17:44:14 ATC No known aircraft in the vicinity.

17:44:25 COP Check its speed . . . it's ### moving faster than we are.

17:44:44 CA That's impossible. Tower, aircraft now rising toward us at speed.

17:45:16 ATC Confirm you cannot identify aircraft.

17:45:23 CA Affirmative.

17:46:12 COP Cam, that's no ### aircraft! Its wings are . . . flapping.

17:46:35 CA It's flying over us. My God! Look at the size of it! Tower, not—repeat *not*—an aircraft . . . It's . . . it's . . .

17:47:39 CA Tower, UFO is . . . is . . . well, ###. What do you think, Dave?

17:48:00 COP Um, pterodactyl? Pterosaur? Flying . . . um . . . lizard . . . ?

17:48:10 ATC ZULU ALPHA, please repeat sighting.

17:48:17 CA Oh my God! It's holding a pattern directly in front of us! Its eyes . . . burning . . . burning . . . into . . . my . . . mind . . . !

17:48:26 ATC ZULA ALPHA, I repeat, confirm sighting.

17:48:36 COP Cam . . . no . . . no! What the ### are you doing?! You're taking us into a dive . . . ! Pull up! Pull up!

17:49:02 COP Mayday! Mayday! Tower, we have an emergency! The pilot has gone . . . crazy!

17:49:20 CA Must . . . die . . . Kongamato demands sacrifice . . .

17:49:59 COP Cameron, for ### sake, we're gonna crash! We're gonna . . .

[TRANSMISSION ENDS]

KONGAMATO FACT FILE

Location: Africa, South and North America
Appearance: Giant pterosaur with glowing eyes!
Strength: Can carry off adult humans!
Weaknesses: So far, no one has managed to capture—let alone kill—one, so your guess is as good as ours!
Powers: Flight. (Duh!) Bioluminescence. Death stare.
Fear Factor: 73.2

MONEY-SAVING IDEA WITH KONGAMATO

Use its bioluminescence power in the evenings to light your house and save on the electric bills!

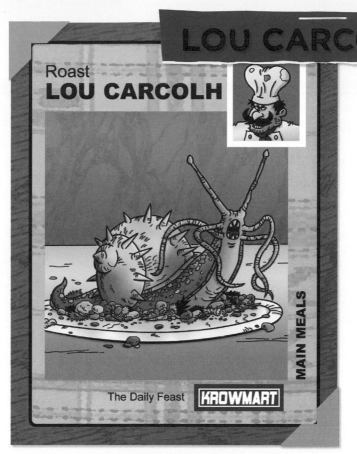

Roast
LOU CARCOLH

MAIN MEALS

The Daily Feast **KROWMART**

From a giant flying lizard to an equally giant and terrifying . . . um . . . snail.

No, don't laugh. You only have to check out your mom's prize vegetable patch to see the psychotic destruction even a munchkin gastropod can achieve in a single night's deadly assault.

And a gargantuan mollusk is even more deadly!

(Nature note: There are over 65,000 different types of gastropods, including land, sea, and freshwater snails and slugs, and freshwater limpets. They belong to the phylum [taxonomic rank] of Mollusca, which also includes the likes of cuttlefish, squid, octopus, cockles, scallops, clams, mussels, and oysters.)

Set your GPS coordinates for N 43.55087, E -0.98476. Postal code: 40300. You'll find yourself in the quaint French village of Hastingues (population 510—yeah, we're talking mondo small!) in the district of Landes in the Aquitaine region.

(Geography note: The *bastide*—a fortified walled town—of Hastingues was founded in 1289, but the town wall still hadn't been finished by the fifteenth century!)

Nicknamed Lou Carcolh (the Snail), visitors mistakenly believe that the village's cutesy-poo sobriquet (nickname) comes from being positioned atop a huge, round hill.

Uh-uh! Nope! The name actually refers to the ginormous, carnivorous, human-eating snail that lives in the subterranean caverns beneath the hill!

Lou Carcolh's size dwarfs by a kazillion that of the African *Achatina achatina* (aka tiger snail and/or giant Ghana snail), whose shell length of approximately seven inches makes it the world's largest land snail.

(Largest marine snail? That would be *Syrinx aruanus*, better known as the Australian trumpet or false trumpet, which hits the length of 35.8 inches and weighs in at an eye-popping forty pounds!)

Ha! Pipsqueaks! Louie's shell is almost as big as the hill itself!

Its body is described as serpentine in appearance, extremely long and boneless and totally gruesome!

You know that disgusting snot-slime that garden snails leave behind? Well, Louie poos out the stuff on the ground close to the entrance of its cave.

When some poor sap steps on the goo, they find themselves stuck fast! It is then that Lou Carcolh—strikes!

Surrounding its huge mouth, which is filled with serrated teeth, are hairy, slimy tentacles that stretch out literally for miles! Once prey is sighted—animal or human—the tentacles shoot forward, wrapping around the hapless victim, who is pulled screaming into Lou Carcolh's mouth to be swallowed whole!

Case Study 187/9LC

Some so-called "gastronomes" (supposed "connoisseurs" of good food and drink—yeah, right!) have truly disgusting eating habits.

Such as? One "specialty of the day" is called foie gras (French for "fatty liver"), which involves painfully shoving a plastic or metal tube down the throat of a living goose or duck and violently force-feeding the poor creature until its liver expands to up to ten times the normal size.

It then has its throat cut, and the by-now diseased liver is cut out to sell to eager gourmets. Lovely.

And let's not forget that twisted oddity of chewing on dead snails! Eww!

This involves collecting land snails and boiling them alive, before removing them from their shells and gutting them. The eviscerated remains are cooked in garlic butter, chicken stock, or wine.

Finally, the snails' withered bodies are stuffed back inside their shells and served as a starter before the main meal. Yum!

The American multinational retail corporation Krowmart has recently launched a series of avant-garde recipe cards created by famous French chef Pierre le Soufflé.

(Vocabulary note: Avant-garde is French for vanguard and is given to people, ideas, and methods that are new or experimental in nature.)

Check out Pierre's recipe for escargot de Lou Carcolh!

Ingrédients

Un mort Lou Carcolh, retiré de shell (One dead Lou Carcolh, removed from shell)
Trois cents bâtons de beurre (300 sticks of butter)
Cent échalotes (100 shallots)
Cent vingt gousses d'ail (120 cloves of garlic)
Un camion rempli de persil (A truck filled with parsley)
Quinze bouteilles de jus de citron frais (15 bottles of fresh lemon juice)
Ciment mélange de sel et de poivre (Cement mixture of salt and pepper)

Mode d'emploi

Build clay oven the size of *une grande colline* (a large hillside), then set aside *a sec* (to dry).

Rinse *l'escargot* (the snail) under warm water from *un arrosage* (a water hose). Pat shell dry with *un géant serviette en papier* (a giant paper towel).

In *un gigantesque bol à mélanger* (a giant mixing bowl) combine *tous les ingrédients*—oui, à la fois! (all the ingredients—yes, at once!)—and mix well using a giant tunneling machine.

Scoop half *le mélange* (the mixture) into empty snail shell using *une grande pelle* (a large shovel). Stuff *les morts escargot* (the dead snail) back into the shell with the help of a bulldozer. Plug *le reste du shell* (the rest of the shell) with the remaining mixture.

Place the stuffed shell onto *un géant ice cube* (a giant ice cube) for approximately *trois jours* (three days) to allow butter mixture to thicken. Meanwhile, heat the oven to 1,350 degrees. Transfer the shell into the oven *et laissez cuire pendant deux jours* (and cook for two days).

Serve *l'escargot* in *une piscine* (a swimming pool) filled with *un vin rouge et sauce tomate* (a red wine and tomato sauce).

Bon appétit!

LOU CARCOLH FACT FILE

Location: The village of Hastingues, France
Appearance: Behemoth land snail!
Strength: Herculean!
Weaknesses: Slow as a . . . um . . . snail . . . !
Powers: Supersticky slime!
Fear Factor: For the kooky villagers of Hastingues who continue to live on top of a carnivorous snail—65.6

WHAT TO DO WITH A LOU CARCOLH

Use its shell for a rock-climbing practice wall!

MONGOLIAN DEATH WORM

Cool moniker, eh?!

And to disprove the old adage that "size matters," this demonic beauty is at best only five feet long and two inches thick, but still packs a killer punch!

(FYI: Most worms are invertebrate—lacking a backbone—the largest of which is the colossus of the worm world, the carnivorous marine bootlace worm, *Lineus longissimus*, which can reach a length of approximately 180 feet!)

Hiding under the burning sands of the inhospitable southern Gobi desert, the Mongolian Death Worm (its name in various Mongolian tongues means "large intestine worm," so called because it resembles a cow's bloodred intestines—*bleh*!) utterly terrorizes the nomadic tribes who live there.

If you're planning to hunt down this eyeless beauty, take note: the Gobi, the world's fifth-largest and least explored desert, stretches 500,000 square miles across northern and northwestern China and southern Mongolia in Asia. Temperatures range from a sweltering 122°F in summer to a brutal -40°F in winter!

The best time to find the MDW is during the rainy season of June and July, when it pops back up to the surface to escape the soggy underground.

But beware! It possesses some totally awesome superpowers!

For starters, venomous spines on the front end and back, the poisonous skin of which the slightest touch can instantly kill a grown man, and—razor-sharp teeth!

It can also squirt out highly corrosive sulfuric acid from mouth and anus that immediately dissolves flesh! And—get this!—release death-dealing electric bolts over a wide area! Bodacious!

Waiting patiently for prey to unwittingly approach, the MDW rises out of the sand to spit burning acid into its victims' faces! If it misses, it simply zaps 'em dead!

There have been numerous expeditions to capture this dread monster.

Its existence was first publicized by American naturalist, paleontologist, explorer, and adventurer (they don't make 'em like that anymore!) Roy Chapman Andrews (1884–1960), in his 1926 book *On the Trail of Ancient Man*. (Andrews is apparently the inspiration for filmmakers Steven Spielberg and George Lucas's action-adventure character Indiana Jones!)

And being the monster celeb that it is, the MDW has even appeared on the National Geographic Channel! So remember to pack your autograph book!

Case Study 741/9MDW

After being sacked by the British Museum (see our awesome companion book Demons and Elementals for all the gory details!) Aussie archaeologist Professor Diggum Upp decided to follow in the footsteps of his hero, Roy Chapman Andrews, and become an explorer and adventurer.

Here is a recording he made on his smartphone while traveling across the Gobi desert in search of dinosaur bones!

>CLICK<

G'day? G'day?! Stone me, is this daggy gadget even switched on? Testing . . . testing . . .

(unintelligible murmurings)

What's that, Abdul? That there red light means we're recordin'? Well, tie me kangaroo down, sport! I'm a right galah! *(chuckles)*

Okay, you beauties, so we're up the donga in dump creek without a paddle, somewhere in this inhospitable hellhole called the Gobi.

Me ol' mate Professor Andrews was 'ere on July 13, 1923, when strewth, if he didn't stumble upon a nest o' *Oviraptor* dinosaur eggs, fair dinkum!

So I've decided to give a fair crack o' the whip at findin' some dino bones fer meself!

Hiring some local as me jolly swagman, I've been t' the back 'o Bourke these past three days an' found nothin'!

But Diggum ain't one to flog the cat, so with Abdul I've been walkabout close to camp an' I'll be a monkey's uncle if we ain't found summat!

A large mound buried under the sand! Could this be million-years-old dino eggs, ya reckon, Abdul . . . ?

(unintelligible murmurings)

(Diggum, chuckling) Abdul 'ere is actin' as nervous as a kangaroo mother in a room full o' pickpockets!

Calm down, me ol' son! There's nowt t'worry yerself . . . it's only . . . hey, do I need new jam jars or did that mound just move . . . ?!

(frightened cries, trailing away)

(Diggum, chuckling) Abdul's off like a bucket o' prawns! What's his problem then? I . . .

(noise of large amounts of sand shifting, hideous screech)

Yaaah! C-comin' outta the ground . . . ! I-it's some sorta great wormy thing doin' his block! *(hideous screeches)*

Fair go, ya blodger, while I grab a pic! >CLICK<

Holy moly! The rotten drongo's spittin' yellow spew on me new boots . . . ! Aahh! It's burnin' through 'em! Yeeoowch!

Now the mongrel's glowin' bright blue . . . ! *(loud electrical charges)*

Ouch! Oooh! It's shootin' out electric bolts! Ahhh! Me bum! It's on fire! I'm outta here before I cark it! Ahhhhh . . . ! *(Diggum's cries, trailing off)*

HOW TO SPEAK LIKE AN AUSSIE

G'day: Hello

Daggy: Useless

Galah: Idiot

Up the donga: Out in the country

In dump creek without a paddle: In big trouble

Strewth: Goodness me

Fair dinkum: True

Swagman: Companion

Back of Bourke: A long way

Flog the cat: Feel sorry for oneself

Nowt: Nothing

Jam jars: Thick spectacles

Off like a bucket of prawn: To run away at speed

Doing his block: Getting angry

Fair go: To be given a chance

Blodger/drongo/mongrel: A not-very-nice person

To cark it: To die

MONGOLIAN DEATH WORM FACT FILE

Location: Gobi desert, Asia
Appearance: Gruesome bloodred giant worm with teeth! (And a sore anus! Hey, you try squirting sulfuric acid outta your butt and see how much it hurts! Eye-watering to the max, we'd imagine!)
Strength: Giant worm-y!
Weaknesses: You tell us! (If you survive the experience!)
Powers: Spits or squirts sulfuric acid. Electric bolt zap attack!
Fear Factor: 93.3

EPIC USE OF A MONGOLIAN DEATH WORM

Sell it to a giant for a pot of gold. He can use the MDW as bait on the end of a fishhook to catch the Loch Ness Monster!

You can't accuse us of not giving you a variety of animal horrors to track down!

A human-eating mollusk! A death-dealing worm! And now—a pedal-to-the-metal, full-on primordial Alaskan aquatic abomination!

The monstrous Palraiyuk (aka Tizheruk) is described as having two heads and huge teeth, two tails, six legs, three stomachs, a serpentine body, and a spiky spine.

Or a seven-foot gator's head, snake's body, and whale fluke (one of the lobes of the tail).

Then again: a crocodile's or snake's head with short horns, long chameleonlike tongue, serpent body covered in fur, three pairs of legs, three dorsal fins, and a whale's fluke!

But maybe it has two foxlike heads with horns; a thick, fur-covered snake's body; two whale flukes or fish tails; three dorsal fins; three pairs of legs with paws; and a serrated spine ridge!

As recently as 2013, a carved ivory skull depicting a Palraiyuk was unearthed during an archaeological dig close to the Yupik village of Quinhagak in western Alaska.

Buried beneath the permafrost are the remains of the winter village of Nunalleq (Yupik for "the old village"), which was mysteriously abandoned around 1670.

Sadly, climate change is quickly melting the permafrost and washing this important historical site—the largest and best-preserved in the North—into the freezing Bering Sea.

Thousands of important artifacts have been unearthed so far, including the Palraiyuk skull!

Bursting forth from the waters of the Alaskan bays and swamps, this vicious and violent giant slams down its eight-foot-long body onto villagers in fishing kayaks, or plucks helpless human meals off the ends of piers!

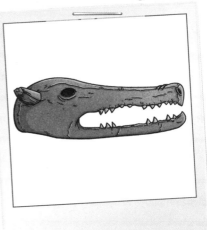

Some more suicidal Inuit doofuses actually tap the bottom of their boat to summon the creature. Yeah, dudes—good thinking! Sheesh!

Case Study 636/96P

Paranoia (an irrational fear) was rife in both the West (North America and Europe) and the East (the Soviet Union) during the 1950s and 1960s.

Each tried to outdo the other with a sharp increase in deadly nuclear weapons.

This aggression came to a head during thirteen nerve-racking days in October 1962—the infamous Cuban Missile Crisis, when the United States and the Soviet

Union came closest to all-out nuclear conflict and mutual assured destruction (MAD).

Yes, dudes! You almost had a radioactive wasteland to grow up in! Neat!

This brush with planetary holocaust didn't stop the respective powers from continuing their crazy underground nuclear detonations, three of which took place by the Americans on Amchitka Island in southwest Alaska during the '60s and early '70s.

It was after the first detonation on October 29, 1965, that Palraiyuk was again sighted. Had the devastating explosion awoken and enraged the behemoth?

One Hollyweird scriptwriter thought so, and in 1966 wrote a sci-fi B movie based on these actual events. Although never produced, we've unearthed that very script!

Here is a sample of that sense-shattering story of the . . .

TERROR FROM THE DEPTHS!

INT. GENERAL SAVAGE'S H.Q.——GOODNEWS BAY——ALASKA

Gathered at the window are Professor Dirk Stone, beautiful marine biologist Suzi Sparkles, and army General Tredwell Savage. Savage is chewing on a thick cigar. Outside, a group of US soldiers is looking out across the bay at the frantic, boiling waters. The chief of the Eskimos is holding up an ancient carved skull of an unknown prehistoric beast. The Eskimos are chanting loudly.

ESKIMOS

(chanting loudly) Palraiyuk! Palraiyuk! Palraiyuk!

SAVAGE

(growls, indicating Eskimos) What's up with these guys, Stone? They gone loco?

STONE

(looks nervously out to the flailing waters) Many Eskimo tribes have a strong belief in supernatural creatures, General. This Palraiyuk appears to be one of those. It's almost as if *(hesitates)* they're calling to him.

SPARKLES

(filing nails) But that's just silly, Dirk, sweetie——isn't it? Why, there's no such thing as monsters! Heavens! We live in a modern world!

STONE

(worried) Never say never, Suzi, honey.

SAVAGE

(growling) It's the dirty Commies, I tell ya! Some sorta subversive trick! But I'm ready! I'll atomize 'em if I have ta!

Stone stares pityingly at Savage. Suzi is now varnishing her nails bloodred.

STONE

I'll think you'll find, General, that is what caused all this horror in the first place!

There is an ear-shattering roar from outside, so loud that the windows burst inward. The hut violently shakes. The three leap back to avoid the flying glass.

SAVAGE

Jumpin' Jehoshaphat! What's that?!

The three rush outside to the sound of machine-gun fire.

DISSOLVE TO: EXT. GOODNEWS BAY——CONTINUOUS

Standing on the edge of the pier. The soldiers are firing up toward the monstrous Palraiyuk, which towers over the town five hundred feet high, its three heads thrashing. Its angry screeches are deafening. Stone, Savage, and Sparkles run toward them.

STONE

(shouts) Stop firing! You're making it angry!

SAVAGE

No dumb monster gets the best of General Tredwell Savage! I'm calling up a nuclear strike!

Palraiyuk lowers its heads and snaps up Savage in one of its mouths.

SAVAGE

(death scream) Yaaaaaaaaaaah!

End of sample

PALRAIYUK FACT FILE

Location: Nunivak Island and Kings Island in the Bering Sea, and Kuskokwim River in Alaska
Appearance: We told ya, already!
Strength: Humongous!
Weaknesses: Knowledgeable locals paint a mystical totem depicting the Palraiyuk on the side of their kayaks to stop it from attacking.
Powers: Dude, it doesn't need any powers! It's scary enough as it is!
Fear Factor: 88

HOW TO KILL A PALRAIYUK

Whisper into the ear of one of its heads that the other head has totally been bad-mouthing it. The two heads will start fighting and the Palraiyuk will rip itself to pieces!

As intrepid paid-up members of the International Federation of Monster Hunters, we know you're just ramped up 'n' raring to go hunt down the most depraved, psychotic, and downright rank feculent fiends that lurk within the caliginous (dark and misty) nighttime cracks and crevices of human civilization.

And have we got a legendary hard-core beauty for you!

A vampiric giant owl that drinks the fresh blood of and feasts on the flesh of babies and young men after first disemboweling them alive! Sweet!

Dating back to at least ancient Greek and Roman times, the name Strix (aka Strige) is also the Latin word for screech owl, one of over two hundred different species of true owl (scientific taxonomic family *Strigidae*) and barn owl (*Tytonidae*) that exist worldwide.

Celeb Roman poet Ovid (Publius Ovidius Naso; 43 BC–AD 17 or 18) wrote about the Strix in one of the six books that make up his sadly never-completed twelve-book poetic opus *Fasti* (*Calendar*):

"They fly at night and target children still unweaned. Snatch them from the crib and defile their bodies. They are said to gorge on milk-fed flesh with their beaks. And cram their throats with gulps of blood."

(Not much of a poem, we grant you, but you get the general idea!)

Ovid went on to list the two ways of becoming this bird of ill omen (if you see or hear one, a lover or family member is going to die!): You're either born a Strix, or you're a perverted and evil witch that metamorphoses into one!

Described as having large, misshapen heads, huge talons, and breasts full of poisonous milk, they get their kicks by targeting newborns and young adult males, eating their succulent internal organs—especially the liver—and sucking out their life force.

(Avian note: Mirroring ordinary owls, Strix possess fourteen neck vertebrae—humans have only seven—allowing them to rotate their heads at an eye-watering 270 degrees. Try that and you'll end up in a neck brace for a month!)

No barrier can keep out the Strix! They simply fly through walls or doors and attack their sleeping victims in their beds!

The only apotropaic—from the Greek *apo* (away) and *trepein* (to turn, meaning to ward off)—magic that can protect you when a Strix comes a-calling is drugged water or a white-petal sprig from a hawthorn tree placed on a bedroom window.

(Botany note: Hawthorn is a plant belonging to the rose family; scientific name: *Crataegus monogyna*. Other names include the common hawthorn, haw, mayblossom, and maythorn. Useful intel for all you budding gardeners out there! Budding, plant, get it? No? Oh well, suit yourself!)

Case Study 028/33S

Online protests are the lazy person's way of showing their support for social media campaigns, whether it's to stop ivory poaching or to ban reality TV shows.

All you do is add your e-mail address to the campaign document, hit SEND, and then bask in the glory of being one of the untold thousands who have "made a difference." (Yeah, right.)

One campaign currently online is trying to save the Strix from extinction. The poor, deluded fools believe the Strix to be an endangered species and want European protection status for it against monster hunters!

We screengrabbed the protest letter and reprinted it below.

5I have already pledged! Let's get to 60!

The world's Strix population is hanging on by a thread, with cryptologists warning we don't have much time left before they're extinct!

Mercilessly hunted by stone-cold-hearted monster hunters, these beautiful demonic birds are facing a bleak future.

The World Bank has given millions of our tax dollars to the International Federation of Monster Hunters, who are swiftly annihilating these precious creatures. But if enough of us supercharge our campaign, we can demand and force this genocidal horror to stop!

Thankfully, the helpless Strix have the monster rights organization Save Our Strix (SOS) to fight for them. SOS already has over two hundred members!! With YOUR help, we can call on governments worldwide to stop this wanton slaughter of the innocent and commit to an "endangered species" status for the Strix!

Not only that! Save Our Strix has come up with a brilliant plan that could help increase their number, if we all chip in what we can!

There's an important corridor connecting two essential Strix habitats in the haunted forests of Greece that is on the brink of destruction! Saving this land could be the difference between life and death for countless Strix, who need continuous swaths of forest and trees to hunt human babies and youth to survive.

Save Our Strix and local groups have fearlessly announced they will buy the land and protect it for good, but to do it, they need enough money to beat out profit-hungry monster hunters looking to move in and destroy it to stop the poor Strix from breeding! The swine!

This is exactly the kind of moment the online community was made for——our unique, people-powered funding model could allow us to help SOS finance this crucial sanctuary quickly, and create a fund to defend other important monsters around the world. **Pledge what you can, and then pledge MORE!!**

Send us all your cash——NOW!!

STRIX FACT FILE

Location: The world
Appearance: Monstrous owl
Strength: Superowlish
Weaknesses: Hawthorn, drugged water
Powers: Flight, phasing, blood-sucking
Fear Factor: For babies and teens—97!

HOW TO KILL A STRIX

Fill a baby doll with extrapowerful superglue. When the Strix bites into it, its beak will be sealed shut and it'll suffocate!

TOKYO EDITION

EXTRA | **OLD GLO**

THE ARMED FORCES NEWSPAPER

Vol. 1 No. 76.

February, 17, 1946

SLAUGHTER!

GIs MASSACRED WHILE HUNTING DOWN JAPANESE

From SCOOP TUCKER, Old Glory Staff Writer

TOKYO, Tuesday

The Amalgamated Press multinational news agency today broke the news of an attack by a terrifying ⋯ monster on a squad of GIs patrolling the island of Shikoku.

Where would our monster books be without featuring at least one grade-A freaky-deak Japanese *yōkai* (supernatural monster)?!

Heck, we could fill an entire book with the terrors that exist in the Land of the Rising Sun. Those dudes own some of the most audacious and grotesque horrors out there!

(FYI: *Nippon* and *Nihon* are the Japanese names for the country and literally mean "the sun's origin." This is often translated as "the Land of the Rising Sun." And the reason for this kooky nomenclature—name—is that the country is located at the easternmost part of Asia and so is the first nation of that continent to see the rising sun. The stuff you learn . . . !)

Now, either there are different species of Ushi-Oni (aka Gyūki) out there, or else the creepoids are mondo shape-shifters!

One is a hideous hellspawn that roams the shores and rivers. It has the head of an ox (*ushi*), the face of a demon (*oni*), and a body that can take the form of a crab, spider, kimono-clad young woman, or even—a cat! (Hey, we just report it!)

It usually tag-teams with the vampiric sea serpent Nure-Onna (snake body, woman's head, with or without arms) and Iso-Onna (vampiric female ghost who can shape-shift into a rock!).

These ladies lure foolish mortals to the water's edge before Ushi-Oni rises up from the depths, death-biting the helpless victim with its poisoned fangs!

If you wanna track down the other type of Ushi-Oni, head up into the forests and mountains. A biped (two-legged), it possesses the wings of a flying squirrel, huge tusks, horns, clawed hands, and extreme-to-the-max spurred wrists.

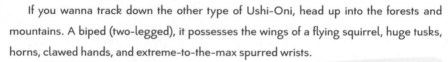

(Medical note: A bone spur—*osteophyte*—is a bony growth formed on normal bone. They are found on hands, hips, spines, shoulders, knees, and feet, and look totally gross. The condition can be caused by aging, wear and tear on the bone, and being overweight.)

Both types of Ushi-Oni are carnivorous, extremely cruel, and savage. They take great pleasure in hunting and feasting on *Homo sapiens*!

Their terrible visage and strength aside, they possess deadly mephitic (poisoned) breath, can lay waste to entire towns with virulent disease, and will even zap you with a death-dealing bad-luck curse!

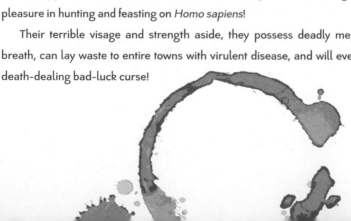

Case Study 475/1UO

On August 15, 1945, Japanese emperor Hirohito (1901–1989) made a recorded radio broadcast to the citizens, declaring that Japan had surrendered to the Allies. World War II was finally at an end.

In September, General Douglas MacArthur (1880–1964) took control as the Supreme Commander for the Allied Powers (SCAP) and led the Allied countries (including the United States, Great Britain, and the Soviet Union) in the occupation and rehabilitation of Japan and its people. This occupation lasted until 1952.

Both during the war and after, military personnel were kept abreast of ongoing events through the popular Stars and Stripes newspaper.

(History note: The paper first appeared on November 9, 1861, during the American Civil War (1861–1865), and is still being published today!)

A rival publication, Old Glory, was an attempt to copy the success of Stars and Stripes—one which failed miserably! Before its ignoble cancellation, it published a story about an attack on Allied forces by an Ushi-Oni!

SLAUGHTER!
GIs MASSACRED WHILE
HUNTING DOWN JAPANESE

The Amalgamated Press multinational news agency today broke the news of an attack by a terrifying supernatural monster on a squad of GIs patrolling the island of Shikoku.

From **SCOOP TUCKER**, Old Glory Staff Writer   TOKYO, Tuesday

Shikoku, meaning "four countries," is the smallest of the empire's four main islands, and has long been suspected as a hideaway for a division of Japanese soldiers who refuse to accept that the war is over.

A small squad of heavily armed GIs were sent to investigate the claims, said an officer at Supreme Headquarters.

The men were making their way across a vine bridge over the raging river in remote East Iya Valley (also known as Oku-Iya Valley), a heavily-forested mountain region.

"Suddenly, all hell broke loose," said Private Adams, the only survivor. "We were almost across the bridge when this dang fierce critter leaped from outta the trees above us and started attacking for no reason!"

Captain Grit Munroe was first to fall, his throat ripped out with one sweep of the creature's clawed hand.

"We laid down a real fusillade of firepower," Adams revealed from his hospital bed, where he is being treated for shock. "But that monster slipped through us like a greased pig in a rain shower. It was a slaughterhouse!"

Soon, the bodies were being washed away by the river back down the mountainside. Adams was the last man standing.

"I sure as shooting hightailed it outta there," finished Adams. "When I glanced back, that 'thing' was feasting on the entrails of the lieutenant."

From Adams's description of a large, humanoid, tusked beast with wings, Japanese locals believe it to be the mythological demon called Ushi-Oni.

Supreme HQ are not convinced of the veracity of Adams's story; he is facing a charge of dereliction of duty and, perhaps, mass murder.

USHI-ONI FACT FILE

Location: Coasts and rivers of west Japan; the mountains of Shikoku
Appearance: (Water) Bovine or oni head; crab/cat/spider/human body. (Mountains) Bovine head, flying squirrel's wings. Whatever—seriously ugly suckers!
Strength: Can arm wrestle King Kong—and win!
Weaknesses: We're open to ideas!
Powers: Deadly halitosis (stinky breath); magical curses; malignant disease carrier
Fear Factor: 89.2

HOW TO PROFIT FROM USHI-ONI

Once captured, sell it to a dental-hygiene manufacturer to test out their latest brand of industrial-strength mouthwash!

Wolpie & the Sorcerer's Carpet

WOLPIE TAKES A RIDE

"A great present for Mommy this will be,"
Says little Wolpie, full of glee.

A sorcerer shouts, "Beware! Beware!"
As the carpet takes off into the air.

His flying broomstick the sorcerer calls
To chase the boy before he falls.

The naughty carpet continues to rise,
And then gives Wolpie another surprise!

In his excitement over discovering the carpet, Wolpie forgets the flowers he was going to pick for his Mommy. "This carpet will make a much better birthday present," says Wolpie, so delight. He pulls the carpet from the trash can and it immediately unfurls, all by

It's not often that we can direct our fellow monster hunters to an actual animal horror cadaver (corpse), but if you catch a quick flight to Munich, capital city of Bavaria in Germany, you'll find one on display at the *Deutsches Jagd und Fischereimuseum* (Museum of Hunting and Fishing to all you non-German speakers out there!).

This rather twisted treasure house of antique hunting and fishing equipment (oooh, be still our beating hearts!) also has hundreds of examples of German efficiency in the so-called "art" of taxidermy.

(What's so artistic about slaughtering an innocent animal and then having it stuffed and mounted, we'll never know. People are a funny bunch.)

One of the exhibits is of a Frankenstein-ian miscreation that inhabits the Bavarian alpine forests, bringing terror to all who cross its path—the wolpertinger!

Although archaeologists have unearthed woodcuts from the 1600s that appear to depict the wolpertinger, this horrifying critter was first mentioned by *Die Brüder Grimm* (the Brothers Grimm) in their two-volume opus *Deutsche Sagen* (*German Legends*), published in 1816 and 1818.

(Literary note: Jacob [1785–1863] and Wilhelm [1786–1859] Grimm were the greatest writing duo ever known. Academics, linguists [those who study languages], cultural researchers, lexicographers [those who compile dictionaries], and authors and storytellers, they wrote some of the most famous and memorable of all children's fairy tales, including "Rapunzel," "Hansel and Gretel," "Snow White," and "Cinderella." Respect, dudes!)

Like many of the *lusus naturae* (Latin for "freaks of nature") that we've covered in this section, wolpertinger (aka wolperdinger, woiperdinger, or poontinger) comes in many strange shapes and parts.

The size of a small mammal, they commonly appear as either a rabbit or squirrel with oversize deer antlers; fangs; large, feathered wings; and with or without webbed duck feet.

Believe us, if you spot a wolpertinger, you'll instantly recognize it!

(FYI: Unlikely as a horned rabbit sounds, a terrible infection called Shope papilloma virus—aka cottontail cutaneous papilloma virus—can cause the growth of malignant tumors in both wild and domestic rabbits. These growths, which result from bites from mosquitos and ticks during summer and fall, can resemble antlers. Experts recommend that rabbits are kept indoors during these seasons. Serious. No joke. Look it up. And look after your bunny!)

Wolpertingers are but one of many such horned mammals that roam the Germanic regions of Europe.

Wanna know some others?

Well, there's the Rasselbock of Thuringia in central Germany, the Elwedritsche (a chickenlike creature with horns) from the Palatinate wine-growing region, and the north Hessian hamster-shaped Dilldapp.

Others include the Austrian Raurackl, the Swedish skvader, and even the bunyip of Australia! Wolpertingers are also believed to be cousins of the North American jackalope!

The easiest way to catch one is to persuade a beautiful young woman to go, on the night of a full moon, into a forest where a wolpertinger has been spotted, find a secluded spot and, um . . . take off her clothes! (Good luck with that!)

The sight of a naked woman's breasts sends the wolpertinger into apoplexy (great excitement), upon which he promptly . . . faints!

Case Study 808/55W

The newspaper strip featuring Rupert Bear was created by English artist Mary Tourtel (1974–1948).

Aimed at lil' munchkins, the series stars a friendly white-furred bear dressed in a red sweater and yellow-checkered pants.

The strip first appeared in the *Daily Express* British newspaper on November 8, 1920—and is still running today!

Unlike modern comic strips, which use captions and dialogue balloons, the majority of the text was placed beneath the illustrations.

Following the success of Rupert, a German publisher created its own comic series featuring a young, friendly wolpertinger. Sadly, this strip did not last long, and all the artwork was destroyed.

Well, not all! 'Cause guess what, dudes and dudettes! We've discovered a single surviving page!

Don't thank us—the bill's in the mail!

WOLPIE & THE SORCERER'S CARPET: WOLPIE TAKES A RIDE

In his excitement over discovering the carpet, Wolpie forgets the flowers he was going to pick for his mommy. "This carpet will make a much better birthday present," says Wolpie, squealing with delight. He pulls the carpet from the trash can and it immediately unfurls, all by itself! "What lovely colors!" Wolpie cries, stepping onto the carpet. "And so soft!" A gruff-looking man with a long white beard, pointed hat, and strange clothes rushes out of his house. "Don't stand on that carpet!" he shouts in warning, startling poor Wolpie. "It's magic!" Too late! The carpet lifts off into the air, taking the young wolpertinger with it. "Waaah! Let me down!" he wails, falling to his knees and gripping tightly to the carpet's edges. The carpet climbs higher and higher! "Of dash and bother!" says the man, who is actually a clever sorcerer. He waves his wand and a broomstick appears. POOF! Leaping aboard, he commands: "Follow that carpet!" The broomstick takes off into the air! Whooosssh! Already the carpet has flown higher than the clouds! "I want my mommy!" sobs a frightened Wolpie. The carpet loops-the-loop, making Wolpie scream——and then he falls off!

WOLPERTINGER FACT FILE

Location: Bavaria, Germany
Appearance: Small, cute mammal with antlers, wings, and webbed feet
Strength: Puny!
Weaknesses: Naked women!
Powers: The power to make monster hunters laugh out loud!
Fear Factor: 3

ONCE YOU'VE CAUGHT A WOLPERTINGER . . .

Use him to play a hilarious trick on the local vet! They'll be baffled for days!

ANIMAL HORRORS FACT FILES

AL-MI'RAJ

Location: The supposedly "mythical" island of Jezîrat al-Tennyn in the Indian Ocean. The ocean, the world's third-largest, makes up approximately 20 percent of the water on the planet, and may also be home to the "mythical" continent of Lemuria.

Appearance: Oversize yellow rabbit (don't laugh!) with a two-foot black spiral horn sticking out of its forehead

Strength: Ferocious (for a rabbit)

Weaknesses: Poisoned carrots! (Poisoned *anything*, actually!)

Powers: Kills large animals and humans with its deadly horn and then devours them!

Fear Factor: 16.1

BASAN

(aka Basabasa—Japanese for "rustling"; Inuhoo)

Location: The mountainous bamboo groves of the Ehime Prefecture on the island of Shikoku, Japan

Appearance: Oversize chicken with bright-red crest. Nocturnal.

Strength: Um, it's a big ghost chicken!

Weaknesses: Its "power" (see below) can't actually do anything! If seen by a human, a Basan simply vanishes. (Good luck catching one!)

Powers: Breathes a deathly cold red (but harmless) ghost-fire from its mouth!

Fear Factor: -21 (So totally safe for all you neo-monster hunters out there!)

CADEJO

Location: Graveyards and dark alleys in southern Mexico and Central America, specifically Belize, Costa Rica, Guatemala, Honduras, and Nicaragua
Appearance: Cow-size white or black dog-goat-bull combo with a shimmering, short, shaggy coat and burning red eyes. Stinks of fresh urine and sulfur. Usually the black cadejo is evil, but not always—so beware! There are three types: (1) the devil himself in disguise, usually carrying red-hot chains bound around his feet; (2) the regular cadejo; (3) a cadejo-dog hybrid.
Strength: Phenomenal!
Weaknesses: The first two types are impossible to defeat. The third is mortal and can be killed like any normal animal. Religious artifacts and burning incense will frighten away all three.
Powers: Immortality (the first two types), superstrength, hypnotism, paralyzing stare, bad-luck curse; one glimpse of a cadejo will drive you forever gaga!
Fear Factor: 83.9

FLITTERBICK

Location: Forests of North America
Appearance: Oversize squirrel with wings. (Nature note: Squirrels have existed since the Eocene Epoch, which lasted from 41.3 to 33.7 million years ago, give or take a month. They belong to the family *Sciuridae* and include all types of squirrels, chipmunks, marmots, and prairie dogs.)
Strength: Squirrelly
Weaknesses: Accidentally kills—and dies—by crashing at superspeed into passing humans
Powers: Flies so fast as to become invisible to the eye
Fear Factor: 4.7. This guy's harmless enough—just duck when you hear something invisible whizzing toward your head!

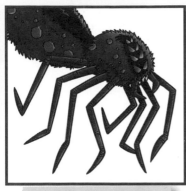

GIANT SPIDERS

Location: Worldwide (Nature note: More than 43,000 different species have so far been discovered, the first of which appeared during the Devonian Period, around 386 million years ago.)

Appearance: Hideous, giant (some as big as mountains!) eight-legged beasties whose fangs drip acidic and poisonous venom! (Not to be confused with the harmless ones you find in the bathtub!)

Strength: Terrifying!

Weaknesses: A nuclear missile should do the trick, if you have one handy!

Powers: Superspeed; deadly venom; they spin unbreakable silk webs to catch human prey!

Fear Factor: If you meet one and you suffer from arachnophobia—a fear of spiders—100,000!!! Aaaaaaaaaah!!!

LAU

Location: The swamps around Lake No, Sudan, East Africa

Appearance: Anywhere from twelve to one hundred feet long; donkey-shaped, elongated serpent body; flippers; yellowish-brown skin; extremely long tentacles hanging from the muzzle.
Similar in appearance to the aquatic dinosaur the elasmosaurus (cousin to the plesiosaurus), which hung around on street corners 80.5 million years ago during the Cretaceous period. Its cry sounds like that of an oversize elephant.

Strength: Even the little ones are tough, but those full-size ones? Mamma mia!

Weaknesses: Spears, bullets, grenades, mankind's usual killing weapons

Powers: Uses tentacles to snare prey, especially humans

Fear Factor: 30

PIASA

Location: Mississippi River near Alton, Illinois
Appearance: Giant sixteen-foot bird covered in fish scales, with a bear's face; satanic red eyes; large, razor-sharp teeth; a long beard; huge bat wings; eagle claws; a long, forked tail; and moose antlers! (Friend to the wolpertinger!)
Strength: Can snatch up and fly off with a grown deer, although it prefers human meat
Weaknesses: A mass fusillade of arrows or spears will bring down a Piasa—if you can reach that high!
Powers: Superspeed flight; superstrength; can fly to altitudes of five hundred feet
Fear Factor: 43 (Imagine being splattered by poo from a bird the size of Piasa—yeeuucck!)

ROMPO

Location: Africa and India
Appearance: Hare's head, human ears, horse's mane, badger's feet, elongated skeletal body, and tail. Three feet in length. Nocturnal. Feeds off dead humans.
Strength: Weak
Weaknesses: Just about everything!
Powers: Chameleon powers—when frightened, will change color to suit its surroundings
Fear Factor: -67 (Your baby sibling could take one down!)

Location: Seas around South Africa
Appearance: Approximately fifty feet long, elephant's trunk, snow-white polar bear-type fur, fins, lobster's tail
Strength: The dude was seen taking on two killer whales at once—and he won!
Weaknesses: A depth charge?! Maybe?!
Powers: Superstrength, speed swimmer
Fear Factor: If you're out in a boat and Trunko attacks—78.4

TRUNKO

Location: Lives under the ice floes around Alaska
Appearance: Giant, carnivorous sea mouse with a very long prehensile tail
Strength: This Colossus of the Rodent World can overturn large boats!
Weaknesses: Indestructible! A powerful magic spell that shrinks Ugjuknarpak down to mouse size would be useful. Know of one?!
Powers: Superkeen hearing and speed; superstrength; an impenetrable hide. It whips its tail around its human victims' necks before pulling them under the water to drown. Especially enjoys feasting on people from the Inuit community.
Fear Factor: For the Inuit people _____

UGJUKNARPAK

VEGETABLE LAMB

(aka the Vegetable Lamb of Tartary, the Scythian Lamb, the Borometz, the Barometz)

Location: Countries of Central and Northern Asia, including China, Iran, Mongolia, Afghanistan, and Siberia

Appearance: Okay, this zoophyte—an animal that looks like a plant!—isn't exactly an animal "horror," per se (Latin for "in itself"), but he's so kooky-fresh we just had to include him! He starts out as a plant that bears melon-size fruit. When this fruit bursts open, out pops a little lambsy. The lamb is connected by an umbilical cord from its navel to the plant.

Strength: The strength of a baby lamb! *Baaaa!*

Weaknesses: Vegetable Lamb grazes on the vegetation around the plant. When the entire food source has been eaten, both plant and lamb wither and die! Boo-hoo!

Powers: The ability to make grown adults go "Awww!" and "Ahhh!"

Fear Factor: You're joking, right . . . ?!

ZAMBA ZARAA

Location: Gobi desert, Asia

Appearance: Resembles a giant, inflatable hedgehog! (We kid you not!)

Strength: Well, a giant hedgehog is no pushover! Try it and see!

Weaknesses: Pierce it with a spear and—POP!

Powers: When frightened, Zamba Zaraa secures its tail to the ground and inflates its body to the size of a yurt. (A yurt is a portable dwelling made from wood and felt, used by desert nomads. An adult human can comfortably stand up straight in a yurt, which gives you some idea of the size of the Zamba Zaraa!) Its spines will impale its victims.

Fear Factor: 4